Amelia stared down at the face of the man who was still beneath her.

A man who might or might not be an intruder but who definitely was, she suddenly realized, having a reaction—not to what had just transpired, but to what was happening this very moment. The very intimate contact of their bodies.

The ends of her robe were spread out on either side like two giant wings of a bird, and the scrap of silk beneath seemed not to be there at all.

Every inch of his rocklike body was imprinted against hers. And she was achingly aware of it.

Gastonia's cool night breezes faded instantly, all but fried in the face of the heat that was traveling up and down her body like white lightning desperately searching for a target.

"Russell." Her voice sounded hoarse to her ears.

The smile that slipped along his lips was positively wicked. He made no effort to move or rectify the situation. "At your service, Princess."

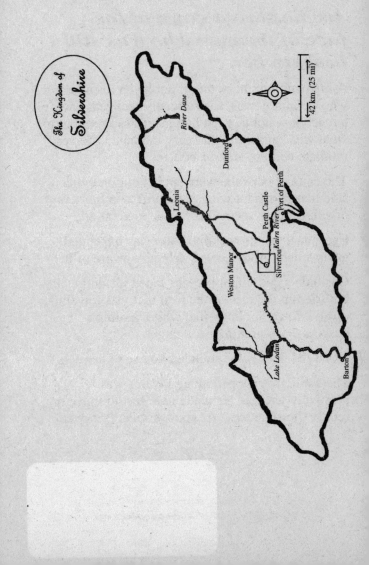

The Kingdom of
Silvershire

River Dane

Dunford

Leonia

Weston Manor

Perth Castle

Silverton

Kairn River

Port of Perth

Lake Lodan

Barton

42 km. (25 mi)

MARIE FERRARELLA

The Heart of a Ruler

Silhouette®

INTIMATE MOMENTS™

Published by Silhouette Books

America's Publisher of Contemporary Romance

Special thanks and acknowledgment
are given to Marie Ferrarella for her contribution
to the CAPTURING THE CROWN miniseries.

SILHOUETTE BOOKS

ISBN 0-373-27482-3

THE HEART OF A RULER

Visit Silhouette Books at www.eHarlequin.com

Printed in U.S.A.

Books by Marie Ferrarella in miniseries

MARIE FERRARELLA

This *USA TODAY* bestselling and RITA® Award-winning author has written over 150 books for Silhouette, some under the name Marie Nicole. Her romances are beloved by fans worldwide.

To
Nickolas J. Gardner
One of the best Test Leads ever.
And to one of the most Incredible teams ever,
Brooks Rowlett, Craig Scheile,
Jarded Hickman & Paul Adriano.
You guys are the greatest!

Chapter 1

"What's the big deal?" Reginald, the crown prince of Silvershire, asked with a laugh that only partially echoed with humor.

The other viable emotion that was present, and more than a little evident in his retort, was irritation. It was common knowledge that Reginald had never liked being challenged or questioned by anyone. His was the right to do or say whatever pleased him. Explanations did not please him. The only other person in the kingdom who dared question him—on rare occasions—was his father. For the most part, King Weston doted on him as Reginald was the single living testimony of his late wife's love.

Obviously struggling with a temper that rarely resided in check, Reginald paced about his bedroom. He shot the companion of his childhood an impatient look.

Reginald frowned, his handsome features taking on a malevolent appearance. "It's not as if I'm asking you to marry her in my place. Just go and fetch the damn woman and bring her back."

"Fetch her." Lord Russell Southgate, the present duke of Carrington, repeated the phrase the prince had thrown out so cavalierly. Because he knew her, or had known her when they were children, he took offense for the woman who wasn't there to do it for herself. "Amelia is not a dog, Reginald, she's a princess."

Russell watched Reginald square his far-from-broad shoulders. Only in the privacy of Reginald's chambers was he allowed to address him by anything other than his title. By the look on the prince's face, Russell knew he was rethinking that. Rethinking everything. And changing. Because someday, very soon, he was going to be king. And Russell knew that once Reginald was king instead of his father, a great many things were going to change, including their relationship. Because too many people liked him, Russell thought, and the prince viewed that as a threat.

It was just a few days before the wedding, a wedding that would forever bind Silvershire with Gastonia, and it was obvious that Reginald did not want to spend the last days of his publicly recognized freedom playing the dutiful fiancé. Not when there were women to be enjoyed.

Abruptly turning on his heel, the prince looked at him. "You're right, she's not a dog. Dogs are fun. Dogs are obedient. Princess Amelia," he emphasized her title with a sneer since he'd made it known that only *his* title mattered in this union, "is neither. And, there're rumors

that since we last met, she's developed a nasty independent streak. Having you bring her back to Silvershire in
my place will take the little tart down a peg or two." A
smile that was known to make the blood of those on the
receiving end run cold spread across his full lips. "Besides," Reginald continued loftily, "I'm going to be busy."

Russell leaned against the overly ornate desk that
Reginald felt befit him. The one the prince had yet to use
for anything other than bedding a very starstruck young
woman who had managed to sneak into the palace as one
of the cleaning staff. Observing his future monarch,
Russell wondered, not for the first time, if perhaps, in
light of the century they were living in, the monarchy
had outlived its usefulness and purpose. By any standard
except that of birthright, Reginald hardly seemed suited
to ruling over the small, independent kingdom.

Russell supposed it was up to him to somehow pull
off a miracle and make the man suited. He owed it to
his fellow countrymen. The question, as always, remained how.

"Busy?" Russ's deep voice rumbled as he pressed,
"Doing what?"

For a moment, Reginald looked incensed at being
questioned, but then he let it pass. Instead, he smirked
and replied, "Having my last fling of bachelorhood."

Without another word, Reginald began to walk out
of the room.

Russell straightened. Though his tone was decep-
tively easygoing, he wasn't through trying to convince
the prince not to ignore his obligations. For him not to

go to the princess in person was an insult. What really galled him was that Reginald knew that.

"Forgive me, 'Your Highness,' but you've been 'flinging' ever since you discovered you had something to fling." Moving swiftly, he got in front of the prince, aborting the latter's getaway. He'd endured enough of Reginald's evenings to know exactly what was on the prince's mind. "Don't you think going to Gastonia to bring back your future bride is a little more important than having some nameless, vacant-headed woman pour herself all over you?"

Reginald pretended to pause and actually reflect on the question. "Well, since you put it that way—" His eyes narrowed as his expression became cold. "No." He sighed, irritated. "Look, Carrington, this marriage is for my father, for Amelia's father who wants to keep that poor excuse of a little country of his safe." His tone increased in its sarcasm. "It's for the people of Silvershire so they can litter the streets, rubbing bodies against one another as they jockey for position, pathetically waving the flag and getting a small thrill into their dull, dull lives when the royal carriage passes them by. It's for the news media, who just love 'storybook weddings.'" His eyes narrowed into dark, almost malevolent slits. "It's for every damn person in the universe except me."

Russell struggled not to allow the contempt he felt show on his face. If this was a play for sympathy, it fell well short of its mark. All of his life, the crown prince of Silvershire had had everything he'd ever remotely asked for or wanted. King Weston had never learned how to say no to his only heir. Sadly, abundance and indulgence did not give birth to a wise, magnanimous leader. Reginald had been the Playboy Prince ever since he'd reached his sixteenth birthday.

But despite the fact that the prince was accustomed to women of dazzling beauty, the woman who was to officially share his martial bed was not someone who would fade into the woodwork. He'd seen recent photographs of Princess Amelia and thought that Reginald was getting far better than he deserved.

"Princess Amelia isn't exactly Medusa," he reminded Reginald.

The prince shook his head. He'd made it known more than once that he hated having no say in the matter, hated having any part of his life dictated to him. And this marriage pairing him with the twenty-six-year-old princess had been arranged years before he'd even known what the term meant.

"No," Reginald agreed, "she isn't. But she is undoubtedly a cold fish, because she is a princess, which means she's pampered. And," he recalled, "she had a willful streak as a young girl. I always had to remind her that when we grew up, she was going to have to mind me if she knew what was good for her." He placed his hand on Russell's shoulder. Rather than a show of affection between friends, it was a way for him to remind the duke of his powers over him. "This will be a good start. Come on, be a sport, Carrington." The edges of his smile became slightly brittle as a sharp edge entered his voice. "Don't make me command you."

Russell's face never changed, but inwardly, he felt his resentment flare. He could not remember a day that he hadn't known Reginald. He also couldn't remember a day in which he'd felt that the milk of human kindness even marginally flowed in the prince's veins. They were companions because of proximity, because their ages were similar and because Reginald, although never verbalizing the thought, cleaved to him as a protector.

That was his role more than any other, more than the royal title that he bore or the fact that King Weston had appointed him as Reginald's political advisor. He was Reginald's protector. He knew the political climate, knew the ways of the people. But his first loyalty had always been and would continue to be to the crown, and so, to the prince.

He was Prince Reginald's confidante, his protector and, at times, he was the man's scapegoat. The latter occasion came about when either Reginald's temper got the better of him or when he got into trouble and couldn't bear the close scrutiny of his father or the kingdom for his misdeeds.

A scapegoat was one thing. Serving as a lackey was another. Russell balked at the latter and this certainly felt as if it came under that heading. Bringing the princess back was something Reginald should be doing himself. To send someone else in his place was clearly a veiled insult to the kingdom that was the place of her birth.

He considered what it was that Reginald was telling him. So Amelia had gained some spirit, had she? Good for her. Russell remembered the princess, a fair, shy girl with vivid, violet eyes, who, for the most part, attempted to hide whenever the prince and he accompanied King Weston on royal visits to Gastonia.

On those visits, the adults would converse, leaving

Reginald and him to their own devices and wiles. Reginald would entertain himself by ordering around everyone—especially the princess—like a spoiled child while he, well, he had to admit he wasn't exactly an angel in those days either, Russell remembered with a smile. He loved to play practical jokes. Still did, actually, although it was no longer dignified for him to indulge himself that way.

The poor princess had been his chosen target for water balloons. Hers was always his bed of choice when it came to depositing the vast variety of bugs that the almost fairy tale-like kingdom of Gastonia had to offer. If he closed his eyes, he could still hear her high-pitched, blood-curdling scream the night he'd slipped a huge black spider in between her sheets.

He remembered that Amelia always looked so relieved whenever their royal vehicle would be pulling away from the palace, signaling an end to their visit. Hers was always the last face he saw as he left the country. He'd focus on her, standing there, beside her father, a small vision in pinks and whites, her blond hair moving in the breeze, her smile widening as they disappeared into the distance.

And now she was going to marry Reginald. He wondered if he would ever see her smile widening again.

That was none of his concern, Russell reminded himself. Reginald was his prince, his soon-to-be king.

The man was going to be unbearable then, Russell thought, feeling sorry for Amelia.

Reginald was shifting from foot to foot, anxious to gain the door.

"There's no reason to bandy this about any longer,"

Reginald said in a dismissive tone. "You will go in my place and you will bring Princess Amelia back. End of discussion."

Russell found his own impatience difficult to bank down. Maybe because, as an adolescent, whenever he'd heard Reginald ordering Amelia around, something inside of him had rebelled, softening to the look in Amelia's eyes. It was a necessary political alliance, but that didn't mean that Reginald should be able to treat the princess like chattel. "Do you intend to be so careless of her feelings once you're married?"

"Feelings?" Reginald jeered incredulously. He looked at Russell as if he thought that he'd lost his mind. "She doesn't have any feelings. She's a princess," he pointed out. "She has duties. I'm sure she makes love that way, too. Like it's her duty." Reginald smirked. "It will be our royal duty to make the Princess Amelia attempt to make love like a flesh-and-blood woman." Smug superiority highlighted his features as the prince delivered another patronizing pat to his shoulder. "That's a royal 'our' in case you think that's an invitation to sample the royal goods before delivery."

Russell shrugged the prince's hand off. "Have I ever told you that you disgust me?"

Reginald took a step back, hatred flashing in his eyes. Hatred, Russell knew, because the prince knew that in a contest of wills or strength, he was more than Reginald's match.

"Frequently. With your eyes." And just so that there was no mistake in intent, he added, "You're the only man I've ever let live who did that." The smirk on Reginald's lips grew larger. "Because at the end of the day, I will be King and you will not."

Russell knew Reginald thought he was taunting him. Russell was next in line for the throne. The rules of the kingdom were such that if the King had no male heirs, then the Duke of Carrington would be the next King of Silvershire. He doubted that Reginald believed that there was nothing that he would have wanted less than to be King. But his ambitions had never taken him in that direction.

As far back as he could remember, he had always hated being in the limelight. Hated being singled out for any reason, for any amount of time. He would have shrugged off the order of succession in a heartbeat, but it wasn't his decision to make. And he was too loyal to his king, and his family's honor meant too much to him, to ever do more than simply contemplate walking away. His path was clear. He had his duties.

As did Princess Amelia. Hers were harder, Russell thought, looking at the prince. At least he didn't have to marry Reginald.

He supposed there was no point in arguing. Reginald wasn't going to be dissuaded from his planned revelry. Maybe the prince did need to get it out of his system one last time. At least, Russell thought, he could hope.

Inclining his head, Russell surrendered. "All right, I'll do it. I'll go and bring the princess back for the wedding."

Reginald smiled coldly, triumphant. "Of course you will. Was there ever any doubt?"

Before Russell could trust himself to safely respond, the prince had left the room, slamming the door in his wake.

* * *

Princess Amelia of Gastonia stood on the palace terrace, overlooking the lush green gardens she loved so much. The gardens where she had played with almost reckless abandonment as a child. While other little girls might have fantasized about being princesses, she, as a princess, had fantasized about being just like any other little girl.

But even then, she'd known that she wasn't like every other little girl in Gastonia, the once-quaint country that her father had brought into the twenty-first century. She was different. On her shoulders was the weight of the kingdom. The welfare of her people. That had been taught to her from a very young age.

And if, by some wild fantasy of fate, she ever forgot for a little while, there had been Prince Reginald's visits to remind her.

She sighed inwardly.

Prince Reginald. The toad. Her fiancé.

Not that the Prince of Silvershire was actually ugly. As a boy, he'd been decent enough to look at. Not like his companion, Russell Southgate, the current Duke of Carrington, of course, whom she'd secretly had a fleeting crush on, but decent. It wasn't the prince's face, but his soul that was ugly.

Amelia strove now not to shiver even as she wrapped her arms around herself for comfort. In another lifetime, she was fairly confident that Reginald could have been, and probably had been, Ivan the Terrible, the blood-thirsty Russian czar.

At least, that was the feeling she always had whenever Reginald was around. He treated everyone around him as if they were less than the bugs that were so plentiful in her garden. She was accustomed to being treated with respect, yet Reginald would order her around as if she were, in his mind, a lowly peasant.

It was Russell who would intercede, distracting Reginald and getting the prince to leave her alone. Russell who reminded her, in those instances, of a medieval knight in shining armor. With his sandy-brown hair, charismatic smile and beautiful dark brown eyes, he had been her hero.

He had also, she remembered, been her tormentor. Russell had never missed a chance to drop a water balloon on her head, or infest her bed with a myriad of bugs. Weeks after the royal party had left, she would have trouble rounding a corner beneath a balcony or getting into bed at night without first stripping off all the sheets, shaking them out and then remaking the bed.

Still, she thought, of the two, Russell was far preferable to Reginald. So when her father had just now come to tell her that Lord Carrington, not the prince, would be the one coming to take her to Silvershire, she'd received the news with a wave of relief, though she was acutely aware that her reprise was only temporary.

She'd always known this day would come, that she would be required to fulfill her obligation as Gastonia's princess. Amelia tried not to shudder; the full impact was only now setting in. She was going to be marrying Reginald. Sharing a crown with Reginald.

Sharing a bed.

Oh, God.

Perhaps if she'd had siblings, someone could have taken this burden from her. But there weren't any siblings. She was her parents' only child. And her marriage was Gastonia's only hope of security.

Still, knowing it would come intellectually was one thing. Absorbing the full impact with her heart was really quite another. Now that it was happening, she felt trapped by honor, duty and circumstance. If she hadn't been born a princess, this wouldn't be happening to her.

"It's not fair, you know," she murmured, more to herself than to the regal man who stood behind her.

Did he feel as helpless as she did? she wondered. Did some part of her father regret having to sacrifice his daughter's happiness in order to insure his country's continued safety?

Amelia turned around to look at her father. "In this day and age, it's not fair, you know. Not fair to have to marry a man who, if not for his lineage, would have trouble securing a date even on the Internet."

King Roman frowned deeply. His eyes looked sad, she thought. There was never any doubt on Amelia's part that her father did love her. And, she hoped, if there were some other way, he would want to see her happy. But King Roman was steeped in tradition and so, she knew, should she be.

With an air of frustration, the king waved an aristocratic-looking hand at her comments. "Be that as it may—"

She wasn't going to make this difficult for him. She was her father's daughter, and well-taught. Amelia nodded. "Be that as it may, I will honor the treaty and my obligation, even though it's obvious that Prince Reginald doesn't think very much of me." She saw her father raise his eyebrows in silent query. "Otherwise, he'd have come here himself."

"I'm sure that Prince Reginald has other pressing business, my dear."

Amelia laughed softly. She, like everyone else in both her kingdom and his, knew of Reginald's reputation. "I'm sure 'pressing' is involved."

Gray-and-white eyebrows rose high on her father's forehead in shocked disapproval. King Roman was an enlightened man, but not where his daughter was concerned. Even though he had given her the best tutors and trainers he could find, in some areas he tried to keep her unworldly. "Amelia."

Amelia forced a smile to her lips. "I will not disappoint you, Father," she promised.

Even though I'm horribly disappointed myself, she added silently.

King Roman took her hand in both of his and then raised it to his lips. "You have always been my treasure," he told her before he left.

Amelia turned toward the garden again. She heard her father's footsteps recede on the stone terrace until they faded away altogether. With a sigh, she made her way down the terrace steps to the garden. Maybe the flowers and the vast green scenery would help soothe her agitated state.

They didn't.

She was a princess; was it so wrong to hope for a prince who lived up to her expectations, not some personification of self-indulgence and sloth such as Reginald? The prince's escapades were well-known. His face had graced covers of *People* magazine, not to mention that the tabloids loved him. She frowned to herself. Not exactly the prince she'd hoped for.

And this, Amelia thought darkly as she picked her way through a passageway where the shrubs were as tall as trees, giving her a measure of solitude, was what she'd been saving herself for all these years. This was why she'd remained a virgin in a day and age when abstinence and virtue were not so highly prized as they once had been. In some circles, virginity was even viewed with skepticism and no small amount of pity.

She'd done it by choice, and she felt cheated. Royally. Pun intended, she thought, her lips twisting in a self-deprecating smile.

Involved in numerous charities and educational programs throughout Gastonia as well as in matters of state, she was acutely aware of the fact that she hadn't really lived life to the fullest. Not where it counted, she thought ruefully. She'd traveled the world over and was still sheltered.

How could she love her people, be compassionate, if she'd never experienced real love herself? If she'd never wanted to give of herself until there was nothing left to give?

She wished now that she had been a little freer, a little more resourceful where her own pleasures were concerned. She knew of a great many high-born girls who'd been ingenious when it came to satisfying their curiosity and their appetites.

But that was just it. She'd wanted it to mean something. She hadn't wanted the experience just to have it. She'd wanted it to be something to remember to the end of her days. And now, what she was going to remember was that horrible rutting animal mounting her. Probably issuing orders to her while he did it.

It made her want to run away. It made her want to have an affair, however brief.

She sighed, shaking her head. She knew better than that. She was the Princess Amelia and no more able to have an affair than pigs could fly. Especially not only days away from her wedding.

Oh, well, maybe she was being too hard on Reginald. Maybe he'd changed. Maybe he had gotten all the wildness out of his system and would be the good, decent husband and ruler she was praying for.

And maybe, just maybe, she thought as she turned around and began to walk back toward the palace, hell would freeze over before her wedding day. The odds, she knew, were more in favor of the latter than the former.

Chapter 2

The soft ticking of the antique clock that had once belonged to her grandmother seemed to fill the spacious bedroom, nestling into the corners and gently stroking the shadows. The sound became more audible with every passing moment.

Amelia couldn't sleep. Try as she might to will herself into an unconscious state, she couldn't achieve it. Usually, all she needed to do was close her eyes and, within moments, she would drift off. On those rare occasions when sleep initially eluded her, she'd employ little tricks to render her mind blank, enabling her to fall asleep.

But reading hadn't helped. She'd gone through five chapters of the book she kept on her nightstand and was now more wide awake than ever. Silently singing the same refrain over and over again in her mind didn't work, either. Amelia felt frustrated. That self-hypnotic trick had *always* worked before.

But then, she'd never been in this position before. Never suffered through a night-before-she-was-to-meet-with-the-man-who-was-going-to-take-her-to-the-rest-of-her-life before. Because that was what it was. Carrington was coming to take her to her destiny. A destiny she neither remotely liked nor wanted.

Sitting up, Amelia unconsciously doubled her hands into fists. If she had any courage at all, she'd just turn her back on everything and run away. Go to America and avail herself of all the wondrous opportunities that existed there. America, where no one was a princess.

Except perhaps in the eyes of the man who loved her.

Something else she was never going to find out about, she thought glumly. What it felt like to be loved. Because Reginald certainly didn't love her. And she didn't love him, either. Never had. Never would.

Amelia sighed, dragging her hand through the blond hair that came cascading down about her face and pushing it back. No, running away would be the coward's way out. Cowards turned their backs on responsibilities and did what they wanted to, what was easier, what was more appealing. And above everything else, she had been raised not to be a coward. Meeting her destiny, that was what took courage. And she was going to have to dig deep to find hers.

Frowning, Amelia kicked off the covers, slid her slippers on and got off the wide, king-size bed. Because the nights in Gastonia were still cool, even though this was April, she slipped on her dressing gown, covering the very short nightgown that she favored. Tying it securely at her waist, she decided that she desperately needed to get some air.

More than that, she needed to walk around her garden, even though she'd just been there hours earlier. The time for walks in her beloved garden would soon be behind her, but right now, she was still the Princess of Gastonia, not yet the Queen of Silvershire. And this was still her home.

No, Amelia corrected herself as she slipped quietly down the back stairs, holding to the shadows and taking care not to run into anyone, this would *always* be her home. Nothing would ever change that.

Of the two countries, Silvershire was the bigger, more powerful, more impressive one. But it was Gastonia that was the more charming of the two. And it was decidedly not as backward as she knew Prince Reginald undoubtedly thought it was.

The strides the kingdom had taken were all due to her father. Oh, the country still had its charming seaside shops and internationally famous restaurants, as well as its grand hotels and the casinos that always drew in tourists by the droves. But Gastonia had also become an important industrial country producing, among other things, the very expensive, very alluring and highly reliable Gaston, an automobile reminiscent of yesterday's romantic vehicles, with cutting-edge technology beneath the hood that had been perfected by one of their own engineers.

Her father was indirectly responsible for the Gaston as well as for the country's modernization. It was he who had raised the caliber of education within Gastonia, funding programs, bringing in men of letters and science to teach at Roman University, the institution that bore his name. Students no longer left the country in pursuit of higher degrees, they attained them here, in Gastonia. And then went on to give back what they had learned.

Amelia wondered if Gastonia's advancements were an allure for Reginald. Heaven knew the prince wasn't the type of man to be herded into an arranged marriage without feeling he was getting something out of the bargain. He probably saw his personal bank account swelling if and when he thought of the marriage at all.

The Gaston was currently all the rage in Europe. Granted, her father did not believe in the government owning the companies within its borders and to his credit, neither did Silvershire's King Weston, but she had an uneasy feeling that her future husband was not nearly so noble. He might want to change that, might want to put the money from the car company's coffers into his own pockets.

Bypassing the main hallway, Amelia pressed her lips together. It was going to be up to her to make sure that Reginald became noble. Or, at the very least, it would be up to her to ameliorate whatever black thoughts the prince might have about raping her countrymen and helping himself to the profits that were being made. Her heart felt heavy in her chest.

Opening the terrace doors, she slipped outside and hurried down the steps. Only when she reached the garden with its tall shrubs standing like silent, dark green sentries did she slow down.

She still felt as if she were running from something, because, in effect, she was, although she knew that in reality, there was no running away from what had to be.

As she began to walk the grounds, she waited for a sense of peace to embrace her. She waited in vain. Peace continued to elude her.

What were the chances that all this was merely a bad dream? That she'd wake up an ordinary person who'd just experienced an epic nightmare? Or, at the very least, that Reginald had changed his mind about marrying her, or, better still, had gotten lost forever while on some safari deep in the heart of the African jungle?

Amelia's generous mouth curved in a mocking smile. She was really beginning to sound like a desperate loon. Her fate was sealed, she might as well accept it.

She glanced back toward the palace. How had she managed to get this far from the terrace so quickly? Maybe it was time to—

Amelia stopped.

She could have sworn she'd heard something. A noise. Footsteps. Holding very still, her breath lodged in her chest, she cocked her head and listened intently.

And heard the noise again.

There was someone out here.

Her father had left that evening on business, so it wasn't him that she heard. The king had told her that he wouldn't be back until morning. When her father had left, he'd assured her that he would return well before Lord Carrington was scheduled to arrive at Gastonia's only airport.

It was a little after midnight and she felt it safe to assume that everyone who worked in the palace had retired to their own lives for the remainder of the night. Who did that leave?

She stiffened. There it was again. Rustling. Someone brushing against the shrubs that were directly on the other side of the ones she was facing. She was sure of it.

Since there was no sound of soft laughter or lowered voices exchanging endearments, Amelia knew that whoever she heard couldn't be any of the palace's younger employees sneaking a moment to share the grounds with someone special.

It had to be an intruder.

A chill ran down her back. How had he gotten past the palace security?

Her heart began to hammer quickly. Her father would have ordered her to hurry back to the palace before whoever had managed to get on the grounds saw her.

But her father had also been the one to see to it that she had extensive training in self-defense, telling her that in the end, all one had was oneself to rely on. She wasn't going to turn tail and run. This was her home, damn it, and no one was going to make her fearful while she was here.

With a rush of adrenaline, Amelia charged around the shrubs, uttering something akin to a war cry that had been designed by her trainer to help empower her and increase her adrenaline while intimidating whoever was on the receiving end.

The man who turned around to see her coming at him a second before she tackled him was tall. His muscular frame was clothed entirely in black. Like a burglar.

She'd meant to knock him down, to, at the very least, knock the wind out of him. And she succeeded.

Partially.

What she hadn't counted on was that at the last moment, the man in black would grab her wrist. When he went down, he took her with him.

The air drained out of her lungs as she was yanked down. Her head made contact with his chin. She wasn't sure who got the worst of it.

Within moments of her hastily devised attack, Amelia found herself sprawled out on top of the intruder, stars swirling through her head, her face a mere three inches away from his. If that.

If the intruder was surprised or dazed, it was for less than a heartbeat. And since hers was beating in a tempo that made "The Flight of the Bumblebee" sound like a tune being played in slow motion, the registry of the intruder's emotion came and went in something less than could be calibrated by any earthly means.

And then she heard the laugh. Deep, rich, full and completely all-encompassing. A laugh that drenched whoever heard it with liquid waves of warmth. A laugh out of her past.

Amelia blinked. She stared down at the face of the man beneath her. A man who might or might not be an intruder but who definitely was having a reaction, not to what had just transpired, but to what was happening this very moment. The very intimate contact of their bodies.

The ends of her robe were spread out on either side like the giant wings of a bird and the scrap of silk beneath seemed not to be there at all. Every inch of his rocklike body was imprinted against hers. And she was achingly aware of it.

Gastonia's cool night breeze faded instantly, all but fried in the face of the heat that was traveling up and down her body like white lightning, desperately searching for a target.

"Russell." Her voice sounded hoarse to her ears.

The smile that slipped along his lips was positively wicked. He made no effort to move or rectify the situation. "At your service, princess."

As if somewhere someone had magically snapped their fingers, Amelia scrambled to her feet, vainly trying to regain her composure. Not an easy feat when her entire body felt as if it were vibrating like a tuning fork struck against a goblet filled to the brim with subtly aged red wine.

She tugged the ends of her robe together. Her insides were still trembling, but she noticed thankfully that her hands were steady enough.

"What are you doing here?" she demanded.

Russell rose to his feet in a fluid motion she envied. "Apparently being knocked off my feet by a blazing ball of fire." He casually brushed himself off. Humor never left his lips. And his eyes never left hers.

The trembling had stopped. But she couldn't get her body to stop tingling. This was like old times, she thought. Except that instead of a water balloon, she'd been hit by Russell. Sort of.

She was a woman now, not a child. Forming coherent words should not be an insurmountable effort for her.

Taking a breath, Amelia managed to restore a measure of dignity to the moment. "I mean, you weren't due until tomorrow."

How *had* he managed to sneak into the country? Just how lax was security at the airport? She made a mental note to speak to her father.

Her father.

Her eyes widened as she remembered. "My father had a ceremony all in place to greet you at the airport."

If the information was meant to evoke remorse from the tall man before her, it failed. He gave her his trademark lopsided smile. The same one that had made her adolescent heart secretly flutter.

"Which is why," he told her, "I came in early this evening."

She knew what Reginald thought of Gastonia and the crown. Did his chief political advisor and cohort share that view? Her eyes narrowed as a wave of protectiveness passed over her. "To humiliate my father?"

He made no effort at denial. He thought her intelligent enough to know that none was needed. "To avoid attention."

Still smarting from Reginald's high-handed snub, she looked for the insult in Russell's actions. "Why? Are you ashamed to have to come to bring me back to your prince, Lord Carrington?"

She was being formal. Somehow, he hadn't expected her to be. He'd expected her, he supposed, to be exactly the way she'd been the last time he'd seen her. Sweet. Unassuming. And open.

But nothing in life, Russell reminded himself, stayed

the same. Things changed, they evolved or they died. There didn't seem to be any other choice.

He saw the way her mouth curved, saw the displeasure when she uttered Reginald's title. It was obvious that the princess was no happier about the union than Reginald was. And in her case, Russell couldn't blame her. At least Reginald was getting a beautiful woman. All Amelia was getting, beyond a treaty, was an egotistical, self-indulgent, power-hungry, spoiled brat of a man who seemed too besotted with his womanizing way of life to appreciate even marginally what he was being handed on a silver platter.

"No," he answered her question quietly, "I'm not ashamed to be the one to bring you back to Silvershire. I just don't care for any kind of unnecessary fanfare. Unlike the prince, I never really liked being in the spotlight, however briefly."

The moon was full tonight and its silvery light was caressing the man standing before her. Amelia realized that she'd stopped breathing only when her lungs began to ache. As subtly as she could, she drew in a long breath.

"Then perhaps political advisor shouldn't have been your first choice of a career, Carrington."

"It wasn't. But my father couldn't see his way clear to his only son being a beachcomber. And I liked it better when you called me Russell. No fanfare," he reminded her.

"No fanfare," she repeated with a nod, then forced her mind back on the conversation and not on the fact that somehow, during the years since she had last seen him, Russell had come into the possession of a very muscular-looking body. "Beachcomber," she echoed. "Do they still have that sort of thing?"

He laughed. The moonlight wove through her hair, turning it the color of pale wheat. He caught himself just before he began to raise his hand to touch it. He'd been sent to bring her back, not to familiarize himself with the packaging. "If I had anything to say about it, they would."

God help her, she could see him, lying on the beach, wearing the briefest of bathing suits, the tide bringing the waves just up to his toes, gently lapping his tanned skin.

She had to swallow twice to counteract the dryness in her mouth. It was a credit to her breeding and training that she could continue without dropping the thread of the conversation.

"Seriously, if you don't like the attention, *Russell,*" she emphasized his name and he nodded with a smile in response, sending her pulse up another notch, "there had to be something else that you could have become."

He shook his head. He knew better. "Not with my lineage. Besides, someone needs to be there to temper the prince."

She looked at him for a long moment. There was more to the man than just practical jokes and devastating good looks. Or was he ultimately cut out of the same cloth as Reginald and just bragging?

"And you can do that?"

Russell heard the skepticism in her voice. Not that he blamed her. He had no reputation by choice. Reginald's was international.

"I have a modest success rate, but in comparison, it's still better than anyone else's." He didn't want to talk about Reginald. Not tonight. There was more than enough time for that later. He looked at her, thinking about what she had just done. "You thought I was an intruder."

"Yes, obviously." As she moved her shoulder, the robe began to slip off. She tugged it back into place, aware that he had looked at the exposed area. That he was still looking. She felt naked. And unashamed at the same time.

"Why didn't you get someone from security?" Russell asked.

Pride had her lifting her chin defiantly. She wasn't a helpless little girl anymore. "Because I could handle it myself."

She hadn't struck him as being reckless, but tackling him like that hadn't been the act of a intelligent person. "You're the princess," he pointed out. "It doesn't behoove you to take chances."

Amelia rolled her eyes. Was he like all the rest of them? Why wouldn't he be? she challenged silently. He was part of Reginald's inner circle. "Oh, please, no lectures." And then she sighed. It was a losing battle. "Or if you feel you simply must, take a number. There are a few people ahead of you."

"Such as?"

She saw his lips curving. Was he laughing at her? Having fun at her expense? Try as she might to take offense, she couldn't. There was something about his smile... But then, there always had been.

"Such as my father. His advisors. It seems these days, everyone feels they have to tell me what my duty is."

"I won't," he promised, dropping the subject for now.

And then he looked at her, compassion filling his eyes. "You're not having an easy time of it, are you, princess?"

She thought of denying it, of saying everything was fine and that she had no idea what he was talking about. But everything wasn't fine and, very possibly, never would be again. Not once she left for Silvershire and married Reginald.

With a feeling of longing wrapped in futility, she thought of the past. "Things were a lot simpler when all I had to worry about was ducking out of the way of water balloons and checking my bed half a dozen times to make sure I didn't find any surprises in it before I got in."

He laughed. He'd been a hellion back then, all right. The thing was, he couldn't really say he regretted it. Teasing Amelia was the one way he had of making her notice him. He had no crown in his arsenal, but he had been clever and he'd used his wiles to his advantage. He remembered how wide those violet eyes could get.

"These days, I'm sure the surprises in your bed are far more pleasant," he told her. "And come with less legs."

The moment the words were out, he waited for the anger to gather in her eyes, the indignation to appear on her face. Without meaning to, he'd crossed a line. But he'd always had a habit of being too frank and with Amelia, he'd felt instantly too comfortable to censor himself.

She surprised him by exhibiting no annoyance at his assumption. "The only thing my bed contains, besides sheets and blankets, is me."

The moment was recovered nicely. "The prince will be very happy to hear that."

As if she cared what made that thoughtless ape

happy, Amelia thought darkly. "Speaking of the prince, why didn't he come himself?"

He'd expected her to ask and shrugged vaguely. "He had business to attend to." If it were him, he added silently, nothing on heaven or earth would have kept him from coming for her.

Amelia laughed shortly. "What is her name? Or doesn't he know?"

Russell looked at his prince's intended bride for a long moment. For all his wealth and fame, he'd never envied Reginald. Until this moment. "You're a lot more worldly than I remember."

"You remember a thirteen-year-old girl who was afraid of her own shadow." Her eyes held his. "I'm not afraid of my shadow anymore."

He rubbed his jaw where her head had hit against it just before recognition had set in for her. For him, it had been immediate, because he'd followed the stories about her that appeared in the newspapers. Stories that were as different from the ones about Reginald as a robin was from the slug it occasionally ate. While stories about Reginald went on about his various less than tasteful escapades, hers told of her humanitarian efforts.

"I noticed," he replied with an appreciative, warm laugh.

Amelia felt the laugh traveling straight to the center of her abdomen, before it seemed to spread to regions beyond, like a sunbeam landing on a rock, then widening as the sun's intensity increased.

She cleared her throat and looked back toward the palace. It was obvious that he had to have come through there to wind up here. "How did you get into the palace?"

She watched as a smile entered his eyes, shadowing a memory. "Remember that old underground passage you once showed me?"

Amelia's eyes widened. He was referring to something that was forever burned into her memory. She'd slipped away from her nanny, leaving the poor woman to deal with Reginald, while she took it upon herself to share her secret discovery with Russell. It was the one bold incident she remembered from her childhood.

Remembered it, too, because the episode had ended in a kiss. A soft, swift, chaste kiss that Russell had stolen from her.

A kiss, Amelia thought, that she still remembered above all the others that had subsequently come in its wake.

She was glad for the moonlight, fervently hoping that it offered sufficient cover for the blush that she felt creeping up her neck and onto her cheeks.

Chapter 3

"So that's how you got in," Amelia finally said, finding her tongue.

Strangely enough, the air was not uncomfortable, but it had grown far too still between them. And she found herself feeling things. Things that, at any other time, she would have welcomed, would have enjoyed exploring, things she had never felt before, had only thought about. But feelings like this, if allowed to flourish, to unfold, would only get in the way of her obligations.

She suddenly felt a great deal older than her twenty-six years.

"That's how I got in," the tall, handsome man at her side confirmed needlessly.

They had begun to walk back to the palace, to the world where their lives were, for the most part, completely laid out for them. Where obligations constricted freedom and feelings were forced by the wayside. All that mattered were boundaries.

"I had to do a lot of stooping," Russell continued. His mouth curved as he spared her a glance. "The passageway beneath the garden to the palace is a great deal smaller than I remembered."

Amelia paused for a moment, reluctant to leave the shelter of the garden. Here, for a fleeting amount of time, she could pretend to be anyone she wanted to be.

Banking down her thoughts, Amelia began to walk again as she smiled at Russell. "You're a lot bigger than you were then." *And you've filled out,* she added silently.

"I suppose," he allowed with a self-deprecating laugh she found endearing as well as stirring. "Funny how you never really think of yourself as changing."

Moving to one side, he held the terrace door open for her. Amelia looked up into his face as she entered the palace. "Is that a warning?"

His eyebrows drew together over a nose that could only be described as perfect. Entering behind her, he closed the French doors. "I don't follow."

Amelia led the way to the rear staircase. As before, she kept her path to the shadows that pooled along the floor. The palace seemed empty, but that was just an illusion. There were more than a hundred people on the premises.

Though she sincerely doubted that Russell didn't understand her meaning, she played along. "Should I be looking over my shoulder for water balloons?"

Cupping her elbow, he escorted her up the stairs. Perfectly capable of climbing them on her own, she still enjoyed the unconscious show of chivalry, not to mention the contact. It was hard to believe that this was the same mischievous, dark-eyed youth who'd simultaneously tortured her and filled her daydreams.

"The water balloons were never over your shoulder," Russell pointed out as they came to the landing. "They were always dropped from overhead." His mouth curved a little more on the right than on the left. "I'm sorry about that."

Amelia tilted her head and looked into his eyes. They were the color of warm chocolate. How strange that she could pick up the thread so easily, as if no time had gone by at all since his last visit. As if more than twelve years had merely melted away into the mists that sometimes surrounded the island kingdom and they were children again.

"No, you're not."

She was rewarded with the rich sound of his laugh as it echoed down the long, winding hallway lined with portraits of her ancestors. They seemed to approve of him, she thought.

"All right, maybe I wasn't," Russell admitted. "Then," he quickly qualified. "But I am now." He saw her raise her delicate eyebrows in a silent query. And just for the tiniest of moments, he had an overwhelming urge to trace the arches with the tip of his finger. He squelched it. "I frightened you."

"You made me jumpy," Amelia corrected, then in case that would arouse some kind of unwanted pity, she quickly added, "You also made me strong."

He shook his head. "I don't understand."

With the grace of a princess trained at putting others
at ease, Amelia slipped her arm through his and urged
him down the hallway. If her heart sped up just a little
bit at the contact, well, that was a secret bonus she kept
to herself.

"Because of you, I became disgusted with myself.
With being a mouse."

"You were thirteen."

"I was a mouse," she repeated, then added with the loft-
iness that befitted her station, "I resolved to be a tigress."

Russell looked at her for a long moment. "A tigress,
eh?" At first, he'd thought of her as too sweet, too
innocent. But there was something in her eyes, something about the way she carried herself. Maybe the
image was not as far-fetched as it initially seemed.

He felt his blood stirring again and this time upbraided himself. He had no business reacting like this
to his future queen.

"A tigress," she repeated with a lift of her head. "I
pleaded with my father to get me trainers, not just for
my mind, but for my body."

Short on water balloons, Russell sought refuge in
humor. "So that you could flip intruders who crossed
your path?"

Her eyes danced. "Exactly."

Another woman, he thought, might have taken insult
just now. While he had his doubts about the kind of king
Reginald would ultimately make, he was beginning to
feel that at least Silvershire's future queen was a woman
who did not take herself too seriously. That spoke of a
magnanimous ruler.

He laughed softly under his breath. "Judging from the way that ended up, I'd say you need a little more training."

"I'll work on it."

They had come to a split in the hallway. Her rooms were on the far end at the right. The guest quarters were in the opposite direction, on another floor. It wouldn't seem proper for her to walk him to his room, even though she found herself wanting to. Rules, always rules, she thought impatiently, chafing inwardly.

She forced a smile to her lips. "I'll have someone show you to your quarters."

"No need. I've already settled in." Russell saw the protest rising to her lips and knew just what she was going to say. "I assumed that I would be staying in the same quarters I occupied the last time I was here."

What had been adequate for the boy was not so for the man. She was surprised that he wouldn't know that. "Actually, my father had left instructions for a suite of rooms to be prepared for you."

But Russell shook his head. "The room I'm in will do just fine. I don't need a suite of rooms," he told her. "After all, I'm only going to be here long enough for you to gather together your entourage." Since she'd been forewarned, he assumed that would only take her perhaps a day.

"My entourage," she echoed. The term made her want to laugh as she imagined traveling about with an entire tribe of ladies-in-waiting trailing after her. The very idea made her feel trapped, hemmed in. And she was experiencing enough of that already without adding to it.

"You mean Madeline." Madeline Carlyle was the

Duke of Forsythe's youngest daughter. With fiery red hair and a fiery spirit to match, Madeline was the perfect companion in her opinion. Madeline could always be counted on to tell her the truth.

Russell looked at her, mildly surprised. "Madeline? Just the one companion?"

"Just the one."

Russell paused to regard her with deepening interest. Princess Amelia was certainly different from the man she was betrothed to, he thought. Reginald never went anywhere without at least a dozen people in tow. The prince had a hunger for an accommodating, accepting audience observing his every move.

"What about a bodyguard?"

Unconsciously rocking forward on her toes, Amelia raised her eyes to his, unaware of how terribly appealing she looked. "I expect that would be you."

There was something about the way she looked at him that stirred things deep within him. It made him want to stand in the way of an oncoming bus just to protect her.

It also made him want to tell her to turn and flee before it was too late. Before Reginald had an opportunity to defile her.

But he couldn't say that. Couldn't warn her in any way. His duty, first and foremost, was to his king, to his country and to his prince. Not to a princess from another kingdom. The fact that his duty was elsewhere stuck in his throat.

After a beat he finally replied quietly, "That would be me. I suppose that means there won't be much 'gathering' involved."

"I suppose not."

Amelia tried not to think of what she was saying. Of what her words actually meant. That she was leaving Gastonia, leaving everything she loved for a man she didn't. For a man she didn't even like.

With just the faintest inclination of his head, Russell bowed. It was time to take his leave before he forgot himself and misspoke. "Until the morning, then."

"Until the morning," she echoed.

She stood there for a long moment, watching the man who had become the Duke of Carrington, who would always be the boy who reveled in ambushing her with water balloons and bugs, walk down the hall. Away from her.

She didn't know what to do with the emptiness inside.

"We can't leave."

Those were the first words Amelia uttered in greeting him the following morning as she swept into the dining room. Rather than take his breakfast in the formal dining room, Russell had chosen to take his first meal in Gastonia in the palace's informal dining room, the one that only sat twenty people instead of fifty.

Preoccupied with his thoughts, with disturbing dreams that all centered around Amelia and the marriage that was to be, Russell hadn't even heard her enter. He rose quickly to his feet now in acknowledgment of her presence. They might be friends of a sort, but there were traditions to honor and he had been trained long and well in them.

Taking a seat, Amelia waved for him to sit down

again. Since the king had yet to arrive at the palace, she sat at the head of the table. Russell was to her right. Having him there made the room seem oddly intimate, despite its size.

Instead of exchanging obligatory small talk, Russell picked up the conversation she'd started up as she'd entered the room. "By *leave,* are you referring to leaving the palace, Princess?"

"No, the country," she corrected.

He looked confused. And sweetly adorable. Did he accompany Reginald when the prince made his endless rounds at the various clubs where they knew him by sight rather than reputation? Was Russell just as eager as the prince to have women pour themselves all over him?

That's not supposed to matter, she reminded herself sternly.

But she went on wondering.

"Madeline is ill," she explained, "and I won't leave without her."

Amelia's position seemed reasonable enough to him, seeing as his assignment had been to bring back the princess and "her entourage." Curiosity prompted him to ask, "What's wrong with her?"

"Madeline has always had a passion for exotic foods." She spread the gleaming white linen napkin on her lap. "Sometimes that's not such a good thing." Madeline was up for anything; when they were children, Madeline was the one who could be counted on to swallow a bug whole to discover what it tasted like. "Something she ate yesterday didn't agree with her. From what she told me, she'd been up all night, reacquainting her knees with the tile on her bathroom floor. The doctor gave her something. Depending on how she feels, she might not be able to travel for at least two, perhaps three days." She watched his expression for signs of irritation.

But Russell took it in stride and nodded his head. "I'll inform King Weston to have the tubas put in storage for a few days," he deadpanned.

"Tubas?"

The somber expression vanished as he flashed a grin. She caught herself thinking that he had a delicious smile. "You didn't think you could enter Silvershire without a parade, did you?"

A parade. Amelia groaned inwardly. "I thought you hated the spotlight."

"I do. But it won't be shining on me," he pointed out. "The parade is for you."

She would just as soon have it canceled. But she knew that was asking for too much. Fanfare was something that was required by the people. And something, she had learned, that had to be borne with quiet, resigned dignity.

On impulse, Amelia leaned in toward him, lowering her voice even though there were only the two of them in the room, not counting the man whose duty it was to serve the meal. "I'll let you in on a secret. I don't like fanfare, either."

A breeze from somewhere brought just the subtlest whiff of her perfume to him, teasing his senses. Russell did his best to ignore it, succeeding only moderately.

"Must be hell for you, then," he commented with sympathy.

"At times," she acknowledged.

Feeling comforted by the fact that her departure was postponed for at least two days, and just a tad guilty that her unexpected boon was due to Madeline's misery, Amelia nodded toward the palace servant who stood unobtrusively at the ready. Words were not necessary. She'd had the same thing for breakfast for the last three years. Three slices of French toast. The man slipped away to bring it to her.

Feeling progressively more cheerful by the moment, Amelia let impulse continue to guide her. "Since we're not going away, I've decided to take you sightseeing."

He was surprised by the offer. And pleased. He'd assumed that he'd be left to his own devices until departure. This promised to be a great deal more entertaining than the book he'd brought along.

"Oh, you have, have you?"

The servant returned with her plate and placed it before her before deftly standing back. Amelia offered the older man a smile of thanks before continuing. "Yes, I have."

"Is that a royal decree?"

She couldn't read his expression. It was completely inscrutable. Had she been too quick to judge him so favorably? Or was he just teasing her, the way he used to? "Does it have to be?"

He thought of stretching out the moment. He liked the way her eyes widened when she seemed confused. But it wasn't fair to her and besides, he had no business placing things on anything but a respectful footing. They weren't children anymore.

Maybe that was just the problem, he thought. They

weren't children anymore. And he was having some definitely unchildlike feelings about her.

Tread lightly here, Carrington, he cautioned himself. *This is going to be your queen, not your consort.*

"No," he answered. Then, because he'd been on more than one tour during his visits here, he added, "I'd love to see your country through the eyes of an adult."

She gave her own interpretation to his answer. "Then you have given up dropping water balloons?"

Amelia slipped the fork between her lips. Finding the action arousing, Russell forced himself to look away. "Why do you keep bringing that up?"

Slim shoulders rose and then fell again in a careless motion. "Once burnt, twice shy…"

He didn't bother to suppress the laugh that rose in his throat. "As I remember it, it was a few more times than once."

That it was, she thought. "Twenty-three times to be exact."

Mild surprise highlighted his features as he looked at her. "You kept score."

"I did."

His eyes met hers. He saw humor there. "Should I be worried?"

She deliberately took a few bites of her breakfast before leaning in his direction and saying, "Be afraid, Carrington. Be very afraid."

Though neither one of them had planned it initially, they wound up spending the entire day together. Acting as his guide, Amelia took him to two museums, one devoted to art, the other to history. Though neither had ever really interested him, Russell discovered that, seen through her eyes, both had a great deal to offer. In between, she took him to one of Gastonia's many parks for an impromptu picnic lunch.

"I'm not the picnic type," he'd protested.

And she'd laughed as if he had said something really amusing and told him with a knowing look that yes, he was, and she was going to prove it.

So he ate the healthy-size sandwiches she'd produced out of a picnic basket while sitting on a maroon-colored blanket beneath the drooping shade of a weeping willow. If asked, he couldn't have said what, exactly, was between the two pieces of bread. It wasn't that it was tasteless, it was just that his attention had been completely and utterly taken by his companion.

She charmed him with her wit, with her knowledge, with her laugh…with the shape of her mouth as it pulled into a smile. Over and over again, he kept thinking that Reginald should have been there, in his place, learning to appreciate this woman who had miraculously been given to him on a platter.

And secretly he was glad that he was here instead.

Russell found himself not wanting the day to end.

And in the evening, with a myriad of stars littering the sky, they returned to the palace.

The second they came through the massive double doors, they were informed by the butler that King Roman was waiting to meet with the duke.

"I'll come with you," Amelia offered.

"Your Highness, he asked only for the duke," the butler said tactfully.

Russell expected Amelia to back away. Instead, she tossed her head and said, "But he will get a princess, as well." She looked at him. "My father will undoubtedly say something that will either concern Gastonia or me. In either case, I should know." Slipping her arm through his, she said, "This way," and brought him to the royal study, her father's favorite place.

Her father often retired to the study to contemplate matters of state and to partake of his evening brandy. More often than not, she would join him for the latter. His life centered around his country and his daughter, in that order. Amelia took no offense. It was just the way things were. But if she took no offense, she also did not take a back seat.

King Roman looked far from surprised that his daughter was accompanying his royal guest. Looking up from the book he had been casually perusing, he asked, "What's this about you creeping in like a leper, Carrington?"

"The duke doesn't care for fanfare," Amelia said, taking the liberty to answer for the man she'd taken sightseeing.

The king nodded. "Refreshing." Setting aside his book, he picked up his goblet of brandy. "This aversion of yours, I trust, does not extend to the reception I have arranged in your honor."

Russell glanced at the woman beside him. He noticed that the princess had caught her bottom lip between her teeth. Obviously, she had forgotten to tell him about that. "Reception, Your Majesty?"

"The one in the royal ballroom taking place in—" the king paused to look at the timepiece he kept in his pocket "—oh, I believe half an hour."

Having learned long ago to have nothing rattle him, Russell inclined his head. "Then I had better go and get ready. If you will excuse me?" He bowed first to the king, then to Amelia.

She was born to this, Amelia thought. To pomp and circumstance and tradition. But it still felt strange, at times, when she stood back to analyze it, to see someone bowing to her just because whimsical fate had bestowed a title on her. It could have just as easily been someone else.

Her father turned to her. He looked pleased, she thought, and not at all upset by the note she'd left in her wake informing the king on his arrival that Carrington was already here and that she had taken charge of him. "I see you two have buried the hatchet."

"There was never any hatchet, Father," she corrected gently. "Not between the duke and myself."

Roman caught the inference and looked at his daughter. "And the prince?"

"Is another story," she concluded evasively.

"Amelia," he began, his voice heavy with regret. "Amelia, you know that if there were any other way to secure Gastonia's safety against her enemies, I would do it. In these modern times, there are terrorists and countries that would take us over in an instant if not for—"

"I know." For her father's sake, because she didn't want him feeling guilty over something they both knew had to be, she forced a smile to her lips. "I'd better go and get ready for the reception. I'm afraid it completely slipped my mind."

She'd seemed unusually happy when she'd entered the room just now, the king thought. He looked after his daughter's departing figure, wondering what else might have slipped her mind today.

Chapter 4

From as far back as he could remember, Russell Southgate, III, Duke of Carrington, had been trained to keep his wits and composure about him at all times. Eventually, it had become second nature to him, like breathing. Never was it more important than during the most stressful occasions. To his late father's never-ending pride, he was considered to be a tower of strength among his peers. While others lost their heads, Russell did not. He remained calm and clear-thinking. Being rattled was not something that he could ever recall happening to him.

So it came as a complete and utter surprise to Russell that, while assuring King Roman that no disrespect was meant by either Prince Reginald or the realm of Silvershire by His Highness not coming in person to escort his bride home, he found himself stopping midword. The rest of his sentence, as well as what had come before, had simultaneously and instantly evaporated from his tongue and his mind. Everything had been eclipsed by the vision in blue he saw entering the ballroom.

He felt warm. Disoriented. And completely captivated. Only past training had him closing his mouth before his jaw slackened and drooped.

Puzzled, his back to the entrance, King Roman stared at the young duke before him, waiting for the man to continue. Turning, the king looked to see what it was that had caught the man's attention so completely, to the point of suddenly rendering him mute.

And then he saw her.

His daughter.

He saw the way Prince Reginald's more-than-able-bodied representative was looking at her. While his father's heart took pride in the fact that Amelia was a vision of loveliness that could even distract the well respected Duke of Carrington, when he viewed the moment with the eyes of the ruler of Gastonia, he was more than a little dismayed. Instincts that had allowed Roman to guide his small country from its past quaint state to what it had now become, a country devoted to both industry and the pursuit of knowledge, sent up red flags of alert and alarm.

Roman waited a moment longer. He told himself that his never-failing concern for the country's welfare, his anxiety that all go well these next few weeks, not to mention the heavy guilt he bore as a father, were responsible for his overreaction. The duke was just taken with the sight of a beautiful woman. There was nothing more to it than that.

The king fervently hoped he was right.

Forcing a smile to his lips, he leaned slightly toward the man who, until a moment earlier, had been setting his mind at ease.

"She is beautiful, isn't she?" Roman acknowledged softly.

Like a man suddenly in the grip of a hypnotic trance, his eyes never wavering from their target, Russell slowly nodded his response. And then he roused himself, regaining control over all but what he had just been saying. The subject eluded him as completely as if it had never been raised.

"But that was always understood, even when the princess was a child," he managed to murmur, hoping the king would take up this new avenue of conversation.

But the child, Russell conceded silently, did not hold a candle to the woman she had become. And even having spent almost the entire day in her presence hadn't quite prepared him for how regal, how utterly breathtaking and captivating Princess Amelia could look.

It took effort to draw his eyes away, effort he couldn't quite seem to muster, so he continued to look, telling himself he needed a moment longer just to absorb the vision that she was. Russell made a silent vow to Amelia that Reginald was never going to cause her any pain if he had anything to say about it.

Amelia walked into the room very slowly. Not because she wanted to draw out the moment, or because all eyes in the ballroom suddenly seemed to be turned in her direction, but because the heels of the shoes she wore were exceptionally high. Walking quickly could bring about a misstep. Or worse, cause her to fall down. That would not exactly be a royal moment, she mused, and she was fairly certain that if that did happen, a photographer would somehow magically pop out of the woodwork, immortalizing the moment for all time.

Making her way across the threshold, feeling as if she were moving in slow motion, a speed she was not on friendly terms with, she smiled warmly at everyone around her.

And then her eyes were drawn to the young man standing beside her father. Her heart whispered in her chest, undecided whether to beat quickly or freeze.

God, but he was handsome.

Gatherings parted, allowing her to pass unobstructed. She hardly noticed. Her destination was fixed. She could not seem to shake the feeling that all her steps up until this very moment had been designed to bring her to this man.

And with each step she took, her heart began to beat a little faster, like a drumroll growing in volume, in tempo. It seemed to swell within her chest. She was never more grateful than now for the upbringing which allowed her to keep her thoughts and reactions from showing on her face.

Otherwise, she thought, both she and Russell would be lost. Especially her.

Though she shouldered it well, she had never cared for duty. But in a way, duty was responsible for the moment. For bringing Russell here.

Despite the way she had to address him in public, always in the secret recesses of her mind, she thought of him not as the prince's cohort, not as the Duke of Carrington or by any of the titles that protocol dictated. To her, he had always been, would always be, Russell.

As she drew closer to Russell and her father, she heard the orchestra begin to play. Her mouth curved as the old familiar melody unfurled its notes through the vast room. A waltz. She might have known. Her father's favorite. The king thought she fancied them, as well. And while she liked them, she had yet to let her father know how much she enjoyed something contemporary even more.

Amelia sincerely doubted if the monarch knew that Black Eyed Peas were something other than a vegetable found on a side dish at a dinner.

Her eyes danced as she joined the two men. "I believe they're playing our song, Carrington," she teased and, to his credit, he neither looked confused nor tried to contradict her. "Dance with me." Russell glanced toward the king, who inclined his head, giving his permission. Humor curved her lips as she saw the silent exchange. "I asked you to dance with me, Carrington. You can dance with my father later."

King Roman shook his head as Russell placed a hand respectfully on her waist and took her hand in his. He watched his daughter place her other hand on the duke's shoulder. "Always outspoken," he said as the couple began to dance away. "From the moment she said her first word."

"Funny," Russell observed as their steps took them farther onto the dance floor and away from the king. "I don't remember you being outspoken when we were children." He liked the way laughter entered her eyes. Liked the way she didn't take herself too seriously.

Liked the way her waist felt beneath his hand. "You clean up well, Princess."

"So do you, Carrington." She cocked her head as if she were studying him while the music moved them about the floor. "You're almost not ugly."

"I do my best."

And his best, she thought, as the music began to swell, matching the tempo within her chest, was more than enough.

Russell had had no intention of walking the princess to her chambers. He'd had every intention that they would part company within the ballroom, or perhaps just at the door as they exited. More than anyone, he was well aware that his role in the scheme of things was to be polite, to strive not to look bored even though he would rather have been in his quarters with a good book than exchanging meaningless conversation with a collection of royals who spent the evening vying for his attention.

He would have been more than content, he silently insisted to himself, to just watch Amelia from afar. Undoubtedly he'd have been safer, too.

The problem was, the princess hadn't remained afar. She had purposely remained close to him, as if she had decided that he was her one true friend and it was his company that gave her pleasure instead of any of the others.

Toward the end of the evening, she'd almost said as much, but had stopped short before uttering the words. Her eyes had told him. That was approximately around the same time that the princess had consumed her sixth glass of very aged, very fine wine. Wine that had been expressly brought out to toast the princess's upcoming nuptials.

He had the distinct impression that rather than commemorate it, the princess was trying to blot the moment, the thought, out.

So, toward the fourth hour, as the reception was definitely winding down, when Amelia appeared to be just a hint unsteady on her feet, he'd offered to escort her to her rooms before anyone else took note of the fact that her eyes appeared just a tad too bright. His duty, he reminded himself, was to ensure the future queen's dignity.

When he made the suggestion about seeing her to her rooms, Amelia saw right through the excuse. "You're trying to help me maintain my dignity," she guessed in hushed tones, leaning her head into his. Her words ended in a small giggle he found utterly infectious and endearing.

Tact gave way to honesty. Something told him that unlike Reginald, Amelia appreciated honesty. "I'd rather not see the future Queen of Silvershire guilty of a pratfall."

She gave him no argument. Instead, she laughed, delighted. "Ah, chivalry is not dead."

"Only slightly wounded," he replied as he offered her his arm. She slipped her hand through it. Luckily. Because the next moment, the simple action was instrumental in preventing her from having a misstep end embarrassingly. She flashed him a guileless smile of thanks that was completely devoid of self-consciousness.

Carefully, he guided her from the room, thinking it best not to take his leave of his host. The king was embroiled in a heated discussion he assumed the monarch wouldn't want interrupted, and besides, he decided that perhaps it was a bit more prudent not to draw attention to the fact that he had to bring the princess upstairs because she was just this side of inebriated.

"This is very nice of you," Amelia said as they entered the hallway. The heat and the noise of the ballroom was left behind them.

Or at least the noise, she thought. The heat that came from too many bodies too close to one another seemed to linger on even though there were just the two of them. "But then, you're a very nice person, aren't you Carrington?"

He wasn't feeling all that nice right now. What he was feeling he didn't want to begin to examine. "I try to be, Princess."

"Not like Reginald," she concluded knowingly. Though her path and Reginald's had not crossed in a great many years, she kept up on the stories. And she hadn't liked what she'd read, even when she tried to view the articles in a charitable light.

She was walking slowly, Russell thought. Was that because she was afraid of falling down? He found he practically had to crawl not to outdistance her. And her words made him uncomfortable. His own personal opinion of Reginald wasn't very high, but he was nothing if not loyal to the crown. He couldn't share his feelings with her, or agree with what she was saying.

"Your Highness," he began tactfully, "I really don't think—"

She waved her free hand at him and then swayed ever so slightly. She paused to regain her composure. "Oh, please stop with the titles, Russell. I'm Amelia, just call me Amelia."

"But you are not *just* Amelia," he corrected gently. "You're the Princess of Gastonia. And the future Queen of Silvershire."

She sighed. "Yes, yes, I know." They'd come to the foot of the stairs. One hand on the banister, Amelia stopped and looked all the way up the long, winding staircase. She made no effort to take another step.

Russell looked at her, concerned. "What's the matter?"

"I don't think my feet will go." Each leg suddenly felt as if it weighed a hundred pounds apiece. It was as if the weight of her position was pressing her down.

He laughed, thinking she was joking. The expression on her face had him changing his mind. "You're serious."

She nodded. "Very." In her present state, she wasn't sure if she could negotiate the stairs wearing the shoes that she had on. Maybe if she kicked her shoes off, she thought.

But before she could act on that, she found herself being swept off the floor and into Russell's arms. He picked her up as if she weighed no more than a cast-off sweater. Holding her against him, Russell began to make his way up the staircase.

Had she been thinking a little more clearly, she might have protested, saying something about being perfectly capable of walking on her own. Except that she wasn't perfectly capable of that right now. And this was infinitely preferable to either sauntering up the stairs in tottering heels, or scampering up them barefoot.

Her body was tingling and after a moment, she allowed herself to enjoy the sensation as she laced her arms around his neck. God, but he felt muscular, she thought. Like a rock. Except that rocks were not nearly so warm.

With a slight toss of her head, she smiled up into his face. "I could get used to this. Maybe we should give you another title, Carrington. You can be the official princess carrier."

"Yes, Princess," he murmured indulgently, wishing he wasn't quite so aware of her. Wishing he didn't like the way she felt in his arms as much as he did.

She was going to hate herself in the morning, he thought. And probably him, too.

When he reached the top of the stairs, Russell looked down the hallway. It wasn't *that* far to her room, he thought. He might as well carry her all the way. That left less chance for her to stumble and possibly hurt herself.

Without a word of protest or an attempt to regain her feet, Amelia curled against him.

Warmth from her body seemed to penetrate every point of its contact with his. He found that his breathing was growing labored, more pronounced. And the climb up the stairs had had absolutely nothing to do with it.

As swiftly as he could, Russell brought her to her door, grateful that no one had crossed their path. He didn't want her to be any more embarrassed than he assumed she would be.

Shouldering open the door, he walked across the threshold, then pushed it closed again. Once inside the room, he gently released her, setting her feet back on the floor.

She made no attempt to back away, to break the connection. Her arms remained around his neck.

When he began to remove them, she whispered, "Don't leave."

Something surged inside his gut. "Princess, I have to go."

"No." Amelia rose on her toes, her arms still around his neck. He felt her breath on his lips as she spoke. "You have to stay." Her eyes searched his. "Unless you don't want to."

That was just the problem. He wanted to. In the worst way, he wanted to. And it would be for the worst if he did.

As gently as he could, Russell attempted to disengage himself from her. "Princess, you've had too much to drink."

"No," she contradicted, "I've had just enough to drink. Just enough to bank down my inhibitions." She drew her courage to her, knowing that the next steps she was going to take were right. "To give me the freedom, just for a little while, to be me."

He began to protest, to make another halfhearted attempt at doing the right thing. And then the princess caught him completely off guard by blindsiding him.

His resolve broke, like a dried twig under a heavy boot. Suddenly, he was kissing her. As heat flared through his body with the speed of a summer fire rushing through drought-withered grass, Russell closed his arms around her. Pulling her to him, he eliminated the sliver of space that had remained between them and brought her soft curves against the hard contours of his own.

Desire raced up and down his limbs, nibbling chunks out of his belly. Making him want her the way he had never wanted any other woman. The way he had never wanted anything or anyone before.

Later, when his blood had cooled and he could look back, he would know that nothing short of madness had possessed him. Because nothing short of madness would have allowed him to do this, to make love with the woman that destiny had chosen to be his queen.

Which was what she was. For one brief, shining self-contained moment in time, the Princess Amelia was his queen. Not of his country, but of his soul.

The realization throbbed through his brain that he was going to burn in hell for this. But that was tomorrow.

Tonight he would gain heaven first.

Because holding Amelia in his arms like this, kissing her and losing himself within the act, was nothing short of pure heaven.

Amelia felt her insides trembling like a leaf in the wind. It was all she could do to keep the tremor from spreading to her limbs. It seemed so juvenile to do that, to tremble like some untried virgin. Never mind that she was one; she didn't want him to think of her that way, didn't want pity to enter into this.

Despite the wine that she had consumed, the wine that allowed her to be what she wanted to be, not what she *had* to be, Amelia felt amazingly clearheaded. She knew exactly what she wanted. And it was all here, standing before her in her bedroom.

She wasn't going to spoil it by telling Russell that she had been a little in love with him for what seemed like forever. Even before his lips had touched hers so fleetingly in that darkened passageway all those years ago, she'd been in love with him. She had always known that, despite the practical jokes and pranks, he was a protector. That she could be safe with him.

It had aroused all sorts of fantasies in her young, fertile mind. Fantasies that had had to be put aside as she grew older and came face-to-face with her destiny and duty. She was trading her dreams and her soul, allowing herself to be bartered away to secure her beloved country and she accepted that. It was just the way things had to be.

But first, she desperately wanted to be permitted a single sampling of passion, a single night of tenderness and love. The kind of night she already knew in her heart that her husband-to-be, Reginald, would never give her.

Amelia moaned as she pressed her body to his. Moaned as the kiss and her desire deepened.

He had to stop her. It was his duty to stop her, damn it, not encourage her. Not allow this to happen.

But when Russell put his hands over hers, meaning to still them as her fingers fluttered along his chest, all he could think of was how soft they felt. How delicate her skin seemed to the touch. How completely intoxicating her taste was.

And how insatiable he was for it. For her.

So, instead of applying the brakes, he pressed down on the accelerator and roared into oblivion, losing himself in the taste, the sight, the very feel of her.

He felt like kneeling before her in silent worship. He felt like ripping the clothes away from her body. She'd made him completely insane simply with one taste of her mouth.

His fingers strumming along her spine, he sought out the zipper that had been so skillfully hidden in the folds. Finding it, he tugged, even as his mouth covered hers. The beautiful shimmering blue gown that had captured his imagination slid like a sigh to the floor. Beneath it, he discovered that she was wearing undergarments in the same vivid shade of royal blue.

Stop! Stop! Unheeded commands roared through his brain. He couldn't stop, couldn't pull back. Strapped into the first car of a roller coaster that was plunging down a three-hundred-foot incline, he no longer had a choice; he was committed to the ride.

His heart hammering so hard it echoed in his ears, Russell coaxed first her bra, then the lacy thong from her smooth, firm limbs. He wasn't even aware of breathing. Maybe he had stopped breathing. Stopped, died and entered heaven without realizing it had happened.

The threads of the thong tangled in his fingers. He'd never been clumsy before. But he had never felt anything like this before, either.

"I didn't know princesses wore thongs," he said thickly. Her fingernails were digging into his arms. He could see the passion flaring in her eyes. It mirrored his own.

"And here I thought you were worldly." Her voice, her laugh, were deep, husky and caused his adrenaline to almost overflow.

She didn't want to seem overly eager, but she gave up the ruse in a little more than a single heartbeat. This was no time for games, it was a time for honesty. She *was* eager. Eager to enter this mysterious world that had been blocked from her. Eager to enter it with a guide she trusted.

It was becoming more and more difficult to catch her breath. Her lungs felt as if they were going to explode as she eagerly tore the clothes from his body. Buttons were sacrificed, as was material. She didn't care. All she wanted was for him to be as naked as she was.

Demands pounded through her body as she felt his lips on the hollow of her throat.

Wild sensations were charging through her body, centering at the very core of her.

And then they were both as naked as the moment that they had entered life, experiencing life now, perhaps, for the very first time.

Amelia pressed herself against the man she had chosen to give herself to as each pass of his mouth made the passion within her grow, made the demands become more urgent until she thought she would either explode or go out of her mind.

And then she was exploding. Exploding with delicious, wondrous sensations that rocketed through her body, making her feel as if she was inwardly scrambling for some mystical peak.

Reaching it, she discovered to her joy that the end had not come yet.

There was more. Because there was him.

Chapter 5

The trip from afterglow to aftershock was quick and stunning. The moment that his blood cooled and his sanity returned, remorse and guilt descended over Russell.

Regret did not enter into it, even though he knew it should. But as awful as he felt about betraying everything he had always held dear and in the highest esteem, Russell couldn't find it in his heart to regret the sweetest, most stirring experience of his life.

He was the future king's right-hand man and the future queen's protector. He had failed at both. In the worst possible way.

Sitting up in bed, the sheet pooling around his taut waist, Russell dropped his head into his hands in a moment of despair and shame. The crime he was guilty of committing only continued to escalate in magnitude.

He should have put a stop to this before it had gotten out of hand.

Before *he* had gotten out of hand.

Russell couldn't bring himself to face Amelia. He was afraid of the hatred and loathing he would see there. Not only had he betrayed the prince, but he had taken something very precious away from Amelia.

"You're a virgin," he finally whispered. A sigh shuddered through his perspiration-soaked body. How did he begin to apologize? "Or were."

Amelia stared at his muscular back, hardly breathing. He made it sound as if a death sentence had just been carried out. All women began as virgins. What counted was having a choice as to who would be the first. And she had made hers. She supposed it was her form of protest. She had no regrets.

Please, please don't ruin this for me, she pleaded silently.

Amelia continued to lie there, looking at his back. Her body was still humming. Was this normal? She didn't know, she had nothing to go by. All she knew was that, despite the slight moment of pain, the entire experience had felt incredibly wonderful.

"That was the unspoken part of the bargain," she finally responded, reminding him. "That Reginald receive a virgin on his wedding night." Her mouth quirked with a hint of cynicism. "I'm sure he's already had more than his share of those, as well as the tried-and-true variety."

Russell turned to look at her. He'd taken her silence to indicate loathing. At least she was talking to him. And she didn't sound as if she were angry. He searched her face for some telltale sign. He reminded himself that Amelia had always had a sweet nature.

And he had taken advantage of that.

He curtailed the impulse to run his hand along her cheek. "I had no right—"

"No," she agreed quietly, her voice low, "you didn't." She saw his shoulders tense and instantly knew what he had to be thinking. He was too honorable a man for his thoughts to be a mystery. Very lightly, she placed her fingers along his back. "Until I gave it to you."

The very touch of her fingers brought another wave of longing to the surface. He did his very best to bank it down, making an oath to himself that he wouldn't act on it, no matter what.

He looked at her over his shoulder. "I took advantage—"

"You took what I offered," she corrected firmly with the confidence of a woman who knew her own mind. "And gave me something to remember."

She was being kind, forgiving. The smile in her voice tortured him. He felt torn. Because as huge as his guilt was, as overwhelming as the burden of that act was even now proving to be, God help him, he wanted to do it again. To hold her soft, yielding body against his and lose himself in her. To make love with her until there was no air left in his lungs nor a shred of energy in his entire being.

His. Damn it all to hell, he had to stop thinking of himself, of what he needed. Of his own gratification. He needed to focus on what was best for the realm.

For Amelia. For everyone else *but* him. *That* was what was important.

She was sitting up beside him. Her hair brushed along his arm. He felt heat traveling up his flanks, curling in his belly. Goading him on.

He needed to get this out of the way first. "Princess, I don't know what to say. I—"

Moving her head slowly from side to side, Amelia pressed her fingers against his lips, trying to abort whatever disclaimer was to follow. Hearing the words would hurt too much.

She read his true feelings in his eyes and her heart warmed. "Please don't apologize. I'm not sorry it happened. A woman's first time should be memorable. It should be remembered with something other than a general sense of loathing."

Very slowly, he drew her fingers from his lips, fighting the urge to kiss each one. Holding her hand in his, he looked at her for a long moment. There were things going on inside him, things that had no place in the role fate had chosen him to play. That his king had chosen him to play.

Why this woman? Of all the women in the world, why did he find himself so strongly attracted to this one? And why hadn't he the strength not to give in?

"And was it?" he heard himself asking her.

Her mouth curved as her eyes smiled at him. "Vanity, Carrington?"

His expression was deadly serious, even if hers was not. "Concern, Princess."

"Then you don't have to be," she told him. "Not anymore. Because it was wonderful."

Her own expression grew more somber. She knew what they had done was serious. Not all that long in the past, they would have faced not just censure, but possibly death for what they had done. Even now, there was still a stigma attached to what had happened.

Knowing all that, she still wouldn't have changed anything for the world.

"You've given me something to hold on to, to remember when Reginald comes to claim what he sees as his due." She sighed, clasping her knees and bringing them up to her. "Why has the twenty-first century come to every corner of Gastonia except where it would count the most for me? I'm living a life that echoes the Middle Ages. I'm being bartered for a treaty." Forcing a smile to her lips, she ran her fingers through his thick hair. Why couldn't he have been the prince instead of Reginald? Then doing her duty would have been wonderful instead of odious. "This night may very well be the only true happiness I will ever know."

Russell shifted toward her, his heart already trapped, even before his body entered the bargain. He tugged away the sheet that she had drawn around her breasts, his blood heating as he heard her soft intake of breath.

"The night isn't over yet."

Amelia felt the pull within her instantly and made no attempt to resist it. Instead, she gave herself up to the joyous thrill that rampaged through her body.

When his mouth came down on hers, she felt all points of her body igniting again, like flares being sent up into the night sky.

This time, there would be no surprises, this time, she knew what to expect.

Or thought she did.

But there was more to lovemaking than a repetition of the motions, more than just the anticipation of release, and the first and only lover she would ever welcome to her bed spent the night introducing her to all the wondrous ways a man could make love to a woman. And during the night, Amelia proved to be an able and eager student, not merely content to absorb but to test the boundaries of her knowledge and to see what it felt like not only to be on the receiving end, but to be the one who delivered, as well.

Russell's experience was not vast. Unlike Prince Reginald, he didn't bed every woman with a pleasing face who crossed his path. He most valued not just skill, but intelligence, something to stir him beyond the physical. Amelia stirred him that way. She made love to his mind as well as his body. He ceased to be the teacher very quickly, and found himself awed and delighted to be on equal footing with her.

He discovered that Her Royal Highness, Princess Amelia, could easily make him absolutely insane. All it took was a look in her eyes, a smile on her lips, a touch of her hand along his skin.

They made love several times. More times than he had believed he was capable of. Until now.

Until her.

Russell had no idea how much time had passed. An hour, two. A week. Lost in thoughts and feelings, he had no way of reckoning. He only knew that he had never, ever felt so summarily drained and contented at the same time.

Amelia was lying beside him, curled up in the hollow of his arm, and he could not remember ever feeling as happy as he did at this moment. His heart swelled as he looked at her. Russell laughed softly to himself, his breath ruffling her hair. "I think I might never walk again."

Half asleep, she was amusing herself by playing with the hair on his arm, lightly stroking it and pretending with all her might that tomorrow did not have to come. That she never had to leave this bed, never had to know another man intimately. Only him.

"Is that a good thing?" she murmured.

"That all depends."

She half turned her face up to his, curious. "On what?"

"On whether or not the bed is on fire." He wanted to go on holding her like this, wanted somehow to make her his forever. But that was even more impossible than his sprouting wings would be.

He felt her smile against his arm as it widened. Amelia—how could he think of her as the princess after what they had just shared?—raised her head again, her eyes dancing as she looked at him. "And is it?"

"It was." He pulled her to him, settled her against his chest and felt her heart beat against his. As if they were meant to be one. If only…

"Don't take this the wrong way, Princess, but you are a natural."

She moved until she was resting her hands on his chest. Laying her head on top of them, she cocked it slightly as she studied his face. He felt the tickle of her hair as it draped along his naked skin.

"Do you think that you could find it in your heart,

for the space of what is left of this night and in light of the fact that you have seen me as naked as the moment I was born, to call me just Amelia?"

He loved her. The thought came to him, riding on a thunderbolt. He loved her. And there wasn't a damn thing he could do about it.

But right now, he could play along and pretend that they were just two people who'd found each other. "I could, 'just Amelia.'"

She sighed, her eyes closing again. "Good."

Raising his head, he pressed a kiss against her forehead.

It made her feel warm and wanting all over again, even though Amelia doubted she could move. Like him, she was utterly and entirely spent—and thrilled. If there was guilt because she was promised to another, because she had wantonly thrown herself at Russell, it made no appearance tonight. Because tonight didn't belong to her realm, and certainly not to the man she'd been pledged to from the moment she'd drawn her first breath.

Tonight was hers.

And Russell's.

"I wish…" Her wistful voice trailed off.

Russell looked at her, curious. "You wish what?"

She opened her eyes again for a moment. The smile that found her mouth was soft, gentle, sad. "Just 'I wish,'" she murmured.

"Yes, me, too," Russell whispered softly, understanding what couldn't be spoken out loud, what couldn't be. She wished that she were someone else and that they didn't both have duties standing in the way.

He raised himself on his elbow. "I'd better go," he began.

But she tightened her arms around him. "Not yet," she whispered. "Hold me. Just for a little while longer. Just hold me."

It wasn't in his heart to say no to her. Besides, it was unheard of for a duke to refuse a princess. Especially when he didn't want to.

So he remained where he was, holding her in his arms, saying nothing, thinking everything, until the first flicker of dawn creased the darkened sky and she fell asleep.

Then, very carefully, Russell slipped his arm from beneath her head. He held his breath as he slowly left her bed, one tiny inch at a time so as not to wake her. He watched her face the entire time for a sign that he had roused her.

Watched it, too, because he knew he would never be able to see it this way again, relaxed in soft repose, the scent of their lovemaking still on her skin as well as on his.

Russell felt a pang of longing and sorrow in his heart. Damn Reginald, anyway. Why couldn't the fool have come to get her himself? This would have never happened if Reginald hadn't allowed his appetites to dictate his behavior.

The pot calling the kettle black? a voice inside Russell's head mocked.

He was clearly no saint, but there *was* a difference between him and Reginald, he silently insisted. He sincerely doubted that the prince loved any of the women he bedded. Given a test, the Playboy Prince would probably be unable to recall the names of more than half of them. Lust was his god.

But lust hadn't been what had led Russell to give in to Amelia when she'd pressed her body so invitingly against his, he thought. He had never been one to be led around by his appetites, even as a teenager with hormones the size of boulders. Longing was what had prompted him to do what he had. To give in. Because from the first moment he'd arrived to escort her back to Silvershire, there had been something, a pull, an electrical charge, *something* that had seduced him, had whispered her name in his head and made him want her.

If they had both been free to do so, if obligations didn't bind them, Russell knew he would have proposed to her last night. Because when he had made love with Amelia, every fiber in his being had cried that it was right.

Even if it was so wrong.

Once out of her bed, Russell hastily threw on his clothing and then tiptoed to the door. He eased it open like someone waiting for a telltale squeak to give him away. None came. But he wasn't home free yet.

He needed to make his retreat without encountering anyone in the hallways until he was well clear of the princess's suite.

Russell looked furtively first in one direction, then another, before satisfying himself that no one was there to witness first-hand his leaving the princess's rooms.

Because the palace had had a modern overhaul only two years ago, there were surveillance cameras in almost every corner of the lengthy hallway. Knowing what he did about security procedures, it would be easy enough to quickly doctor the tape that could incriminate both of them. All he would need to do, once he had the tape, was create a quick time loop, for both the time that he and the princess entered her suite and then again for when he left it.

It was a relatively simple matter to erase any evidence that this had ever taken place—from everywhere but his soul. But that was his problem. What he needed to do was make sure that everyone regarded the princess above reproach.

He tried not to think about the fact that in a few short days, Reginald could be enjoying the very things that he had just had. The thought was too painful for him to examine now.

Madeline Carlyle rounded the long corridor, pleased and amazed at how quickly she had rallied. She wanted to be the first to tell Amelia that the trip to Silvershire did not have to be delayed because of her.

Rounding the corner, Madeline came to a dead stop. The smile on her appealing round face froze and then faded when she saw the tall, dark, handsome man emerging from the princess's suite. Catching her breath, Madeline melted back into the shadows, her heart hammering hard in her chest.

Her first thought was that Amelia was in danger. If that were the case, she had no business hiding. Her job was to protect the princess no matter what. But when she stepped out into the hallway again, the man she'd just seen was gone.

What had he done to Amelia?

Madeline hurried into Amelia's quarters, completely disregarding any protocol that would have her knocking on the princess's door and waiting to be allowed access. They had been friends for far too long for her to stand on protocol. Especially since Amelia would have none of it. She'd always encouraged her to treat her as if they were equals.

Rushing through the sitting room, Madeline burst into the princess's bedroom. The same room where they had played and whispered stories to one another in the dead of night when they were children.

"Amelia," she cried, "are you all right?"

But even as she asked the question, she saw that rather than looking violated, or like the victim of some sort of mistreatment, Amelia looked absolutely fine. She also looked as if she were asleep.

The sound of Madeline's breathless question elbowed its way into the dream she was having. With reluctance, Amelia opened her eyes. Dazed, disoriented, it took her a moment to pull herself together.

The fact that she was alone in bed came crashing down on her consciousness.

Her brain replayed Madeline's question as she tried to focus on the woman's concerned face. Belatedly, Amelia realized that she was still nude. As regally as she could, she gathered the sheet to herself, forced a smile to her lips and made an attempt at diversion.

"Madeline. You're better."

The redhead waved her hand, dismissing the reference to her health. All that was yesterday's news. She had very obviously stumbled across something that came under the heading of "breaking news."

And she wanted to know every last detail about it. "Never mind me, what about you?"

For a moment, Amelia avoided her best friend's eyes. She picked at the sheet, as if arranging it in a more flattering way. "What about me?"

Madeline knelt down beside the bed, her eyes searching Amelia's face for some kind of sign that would tell her if something was truly wrong. "Are you all right?"

Amelia lifted her head, tossing her hair over her shoulder. A portrait in regalness. "Yes, why shouldn't I be?"

"Because—" Madeline stopped and tried again, more coherently this time. "Amelia, I saw a man coming out of your rooms."

So, he'd only just left her now. Somehow, she found that heartening. It meant that he couldn't tear himself away. The thought made her happy. "No, you didn't."

Madeline frowned, confused. "Yes, I did, he—"

Amelia fixed the other woman with a very intent look. "No, Madeline, you didn't," she repeated, enunciating every word carefully.

Madeline returned Amelia's look, trying to gauge the princess's thoughts. "I didn't." It wasn't quite a question, nor was it completely a statement.

"No." Amelia's tone was firm and not to be argued with.

Madeline drew closer still to the woman who had her allegiance before all others. "And this man I didn't see, exactly who was he?"

They had shared everything. Intelligent, witty and blessed with a delicious sense of humor as well as irony, Madeline was the old-fashioned sort of confidante, the kind who was loyal to her very last breath. They had kept one another's secrets since before either one had understood what that meant.

Looking down on her knotted fingers, Amelia whispered, "The Duke of Carrington."

Madeline covered her mouth to keep the squeal of surprise from emerging. When her voice returned to normal, she dropped her hands and asked, "That was Russell?"

Amelia nodded. Rather than regret what, in a moment of wine-aided weakness, she had done, she found herself missing him.

"My lord." Madeline stared at Amelia, speechless.

No, he's mine, Amelia thought.

Clearing her throat, Madeline forged ahead, "Did you and he—?" And then she laughed at her own question. "Of course you did. Just look at you, you're glowing. Glowing and naked." More than slightly familiar with nights of excitement and passion herself, Madeline knew that Amelia had never been with anyone. "Was he good to you?"

"Better than good," Amelia breathed. "He was fabulous."

"If you wanted to run off with him, Amelia, I could create a diversion. I could—"

Amelia placed her hand on Madeline's, anchoring her attention. She shook her head. "No."

Madeline's shoulders slumped with disappointment.

Amelia knew Madeline had never liked the prince, had never thought of him as being good enough for her.

"No?"

"No." Amelia took both of Madeline's hands and held them in her own. "And you can never tell anyone, do you understand?"

Madeline looked into the imploring violet eyes. With reluctance, she nodded and gave Amelia her word. "I understand."

Chapter 6

King Weston sighed, closed the thick, leather-bound binders and rose from his desk. Opening the double doors at his back, he walked out onto the balcony and looked out past the light green buds of spring, past the huge expanse of greenery. From where he stood, he had a view of the ocean which soothed him.

He'd been in his office for the last hour, going over the final plans for the coronation. It seemed like only yesterday he had been awaiting his own coronation, now it was his son's he was making plans for.

His reign was coming to an end.

It was time to hand the scepter over to someone else. To Reginald. Unlike most other monarchies, it wasn't death but tradition that brought about a change in the rulers in Silvershire. According to custom, the crown had to be relinquished after thirty years—to a first-born son if there was one, to a duke if nature had been cruel and withheld heirs from the reigning ruler.

That was how he had come to his crown. He'd been the chosen one. Oh, not at first. The late King Dunford had initially favored Lord Benton Vladimir over him and it was understood that the title of king would pass to Vladimir when the time came.

However, as the crucial moment had approached, King Dunford had changed his mind. Instincts, the old king had confided to him, caused the monarch to decide that Weston rather than Vladimir would make the better ruler. Vladimir was too self-centered ever to be a good king.

He'd accepted this with a heavy heart, because he and Vladimir were cousins and friends. *Had* been friends, he amended, remembering the course of events. The friendship that had existed had died the moment the crown came between them. Just before the coronation, Vladimir had disappeared, vowing revenge.

It had been a vow that apparently was never to come to fruition. He hadn't heard from Vladimir in all these years that the crown rested on his head. No one had.

A sad smile curved his mouth. It was too bad, really, because he missed the man and the confidences they used to share.

And then there were the times that he found himself wishing that Vladimir had remained the chosen one. That it was Vladimir who wore the crown that occasionally weighed so heavily on his brow. But that, of course, was only in moments of extreme stress.

He'd tried to be a good king, to do his very level best

for the people. And they, in turn, had been there for him.
It was his duty to the people that had kept him alive and
had brought him back from the brink of insanity, where
grief had propelled him. His beloved queen, his Alexis,
had died two days after giving birth to their only child.

Reginald.

Thinking of his son now, he shook his head and did his
best to bank down a mounting sorrow that entwined itself
with the headache that had been his constant companion
these last few weeks. The same instincts that King
Dunford had once spoken of so many years ago seemed
to be now tormenting him. Instincts that whispered in his
ear, saying that Reginald was not fit to be a ruler.

The heart of a ruler should be centered on his people.
Reginald's heart was centered on himself alone. On his
pleasures, his needs. Reginald took no interest in matters
of state, beyond what the state coffers could yield into
his private pocket. His son's main pastime seemed to be
the collection of women.

And that collection grew almost daily, if he were
to believe the press. The newspapers referred to
Reginald as the Playboy Prince as well as the Black
Prince. The less upstanding tabloids called him something that was far worse.

And this was the head that was going to be wearing
the crown of Silvershire in less than a month.

His hands on the railing, the king closed his eyes,
feeling very weary and very old.

God, but he wished that his only son was more like
the Duke of Carrington. His mouth curved again. Dear
lord, he would have given his life if Reginald was

anything like Russell. That was why he was constantly pushing the two together.

Close in age, Reginald and Carrington had grown up together. But they had evolved into two men who were nothing like one another, he thought sadly. The young duke was serious, focused, aside from his riotous penchant for mischief that used to prompt him to play appalling practical jokes on unsuspecting victims, such as the poor princess. But despite that bent, Carrington had a good head on his shoulders, the kind that came from more than just obtaining an excellent education. The kind that came from an innate intelligence and a inherent sensitivity to the needs of others.

For a moment, Weston watched the yachts in the harbor. They were bobbing up and down in the choppy waters like slightly inebriated dancers. He tried to remember if the forecast called for a storm. The princess was coming in today. It would be a shame if her first day on Silvershire's soil was marked with rain.

If he could have picked the perfect son, the perfect ruler, he was forced to admit, then he would have selected Carrington over his own son. What he had hoped would rub off from Carrington to Reginald had not. If anything, Reginald seemed to be even more determined to burn the candle at both ends, more determined than ever to sow his share of wild oats.

His share, Weston snorted. Reginald was sowing more wild oats than all the young men of an entire third world nation put together.

He had been much too indulgent when it came to Reginald, but that was all in the past. Reginald was thirty, he was going to have to put his reckless behavior behind him. The moment he took on the responsibility of wearing the crown, he would have to devote himself to Silvershire, not to the pursuit of his own pleasures.

And if he didn't? a small, persistent voice inside Weston's head demanded. What then?

Weston ran his hand along his aching head. He had no answer for that. All he could do was pray for a miracle, that somehow, his son would be transformed into the monarch that Silvershire needed him to be.

The king glanced at his watch. It was later than he had thought. For the moment, he tabled his thoughts of miracles and simply prayed that Reginald would show up at the airport to greet his bride. There was less than an hour to get ready. The plane that carried Carrington and Gastonia's princess would be landing soon.

If there was something in his heart that felt sorry for the young woman who was to be his daughter-in-law, he wouldn't allow himself to admit it.

The knot in her stomach wouldn't go away, no matter how much Amelia willed it to dissolve. Not only that, but she couldn't trust herself to look at Carrington, even though he sat in the seat adjacent to hers. Not yet. Not without risking having all her thoughts reveal themselves in her eyes, on her face. She couldn't afford to have anyone suspect that there was something between her and the charismatic duke.

She'd been so very sure, only two days ago, that it was better to have one shining moment of happiness than none at all. To know what real love, real pleasure was—even if she couldn't have it for more than a moment—than to endure a lifetime never having experienced it. But now she wasn't so sure. Because to know was to want. And she couldn't endanger everything she had been raised to accomplish just because of her own needs, her own desires.

Why? a voice within her demanded. Why not grasp the brass ring? Reginald has spent the whole of his adult life doing that, why not you?

But if she did that, if she indulged herself without thinking of the far-reaching consequences, then that would mean that she was just like Reginald. She wasn't. She was different. Better, she liked to think.

As Gastonia's princess, she had the people to think about. Keeping them safe, by means of an alliance with the stronger Silvershire, was her responsibility. She couldn't bow out now, no matter how much her heart longed to.

The knot in her stomach grew larger as the plane touched down on the runway. Her fingers tightened around the armrests, her knuckles turning white.

She was here. At the place that she was going to have to refer to as home for the rest of her life.

For a moment, panic flared in her veins. She desperately wanted to order the pilot to pull up the landing gear and take off again. To turn the plane around and go back to Gastonia.

Amelia pressed her lips together, keeping the words unspoken. She wished with all her heart that life had not gotten so complicated.

She should have never done what she had, Amelia

upbraided herself. But she only had herself to blame. If she had not given in to her curiosity, to her desire, she and Russell would have continued being friendly strangers, nothing more.

But now he was going to have a position of honor inside every dream she had. Almost against her will, she slanted a glance toward Russell. Their eyes met.

Her breath caught in her throat. *Breathe, Amelia, breathe.*

She looked away, only to see that Madeline was watching her. The redhead's mouth moved into a quick, comforting smile.

Madeline turned to look out the window. "We're here," she announced in a tone that the executioner might have used to tell Marie Antoinette that it was time to climb up the steps that led to the guillotine.

Aware that Carrington's eyes were still on her, Amelia lifted her chin and took on a regal bearing.

"Yes, we are."

If she sighed inwardly after the words, no one heard it. But she had a feeling that Carrington sensed it. As his eyes washed over her, she was certain she saw concern glinting in his eyes. She managed a smile that was meant to put him at his ease—and still maintain the distance between them.

As if there would ever be real distance between them, she thought ruefully. The night they had spent together had effectively burned away any kind of space that might have ever existed. Body and soul, she was his now. She always would be, even though they could never make love again. It only took that one time for the promise to be there. To be eternal.

Carrington was the first to unbuckle his seat belt. On his feet, he approached her respectfully. His voice was gentle as he said, "Princess, it's time to meet your people."

She took a deep breath, as if that would provide her with the courage that she felt ebbing away from her. She'd been to Silvershire before, but years ago and with her father. She wished he was here now, but he had made it clear that he felt she should come alone, signifying her new position. She was no longer his daughter but Reginald's intended queen. He was going to join her in a day, but her first hours on Silvershire's soil should be focused entirely on her and Reginald.

"Yes, it is," she agreed.

With slow, deliberate movements, Amelia unbuckled her seat belt and then took the hand Carrington offered to help her to her feet. She tried not to think of how that hand had felt the other night, stroking her flesh. Bringing her pleasure that she had never, in her wildest dreams, imagined existed.

Madeline popped up, flashed a smile and whispered, "It's going to be all right." Amelia returned the smile, in her heart knowing that it wouldn't be. Not while she had to be Reginald's wife.

Turning on his heel, Russell led the way to the plane's door. The steward preceded him, opening it for them before stepping back.

Russell looked at Amelia. "The people will expect to see you emerging first, Princess," he told her.

"Then we can't disappoint them, can we?" she responded gamely.

With Madeline directly behind her, Amelia stepped out onto the steps that had been brought directly before the opened door. Standing there for a moment, she raised her hand and waved to the people who had all gathered there. They didn't look unlike her own people she had left in Gastonia.

A cheer rose, enveloping her like a warm blanket as the crowd greeted her. For a moment, she remained where she was, waving, absorbing the upturned faces. There were all manner of people within the crowd. Old, young, men, women and children, they were all waving at her. All cheering for this princess they were determined to welcome into their hearts.

Waving and smiling was second nature to her. It had been required of her for as far back as Amelia could remember. It was, she thought, the meaningless side of who and what she was. The meaningful part came from lending her support, her name and her efforts to charitable foundations, to actually accomplishing things. But because of the state of turmoil that her mind was in, she welcomed this distraction. It allowed her to go on automatic pilot.

And not to dwell on the fact that Carrington was standing much too close to her, causing her body to hum. Causing her to remember the other night, when she had been alive for the very first time.

"There's King Weston." Madeline said the words against her ear as she gestured toward the monarch standing proudly with his back to the crowd as he watched Carrington and the others disembark. "But where's the prince?"

Madeline's question echoed in Amelia's brain as she scanned the area around King Weston. The tall ruler had some of his key people assembled with him. But the prince was noticeably absent.

This was entirely unacceptable, Amelia thought. It was not only thoughtless and rude, it was beyond insulting. Was he deliberately absent in order to publicly embarrass her? Was this a sign of the things that were to come? Or was he just out to show her how superior he was to her?

Amelia looked over toward Russell, her eyes reiterating Madeline's question. If anyone would know of the prince's whereabouts, it was Carrington. But she saw the duke move his head from side to side, silently telling her that he was just as much in the dark about Reginald as she was.

This was not good, Amelia thought. None of the princesses in the fairy tales she had grown up reading were ever stranded by their prince.

Maybe because he's not really your prince.

The band began to play. Amelia shut the voice in her head out. She carefully came down the narrow metal steps. Despite the din of the crowd, she could swear she heard the click of her heels as she made contact with the metal over and over again. And with each step she took, she heard the same tattoo being struck.

Run. Run. Run.

Except that there was nowhere to run to.

The king and his entourage approached, meeting her halfway. Stepping forward, Weston embraced her, then kissed her soundly first on one cheek and then the other. Finished, he stood back and beamed at her.

"Welcome, Princess."

There was warmth in the monarch's eyes, but there was something more there, she realized. There was just a hint of discomfort.

The king was embarrassed that Reginald wasn't here, Amelia thought. He was embarrassed for her and for the realm. She took heart in that.

In his mid-sixties, King Weston appeared to be in the prime of his life. Distinguished, he looked like a man at least ten years his junior. Six feet one inch tall, with a strong build, he had a full head of silver-gray hair and kind blue-gray eyes. Amelia had always liked him. She fervently wished she could have felt the same way about his son.

Stepping to the side, he gestured, presenting her to his people. "Welcome to your new home."

After a push from her mother, a little girl of no more than six approached with a huge bouquet of flowers. The little girl held it up as high as she could, offering the bouquet to her. There were carnations, perfect specimens of pink and white, mixed with several other delicate flowers that Amelia knew were native to Silvershire.

When Amelia accepted the bouquet, the little girl curtsied, then stepped back and buried her face in her mother's skirt, suddenly shy.

Amelia bent down to her level and said, "Thank you."

The little girl half turned her head toward her again and offered a small, hesitant smile.

Rising to her feet, Amelia looked at the throng that had gathered to see her. "Thank you all for coming," she said, raising her voice in order to be heard. "I'm very happy to be here."

In response, the crowd cheered and clapped. All except for a cluster of people over on the side. There was almost a militant appearance about them, even though they were all wearing civilian clothes. There was a dark-haired young man dressed in black, standing in the center. He seemed to be the rallying point around whom the others gathered. Behind him was a banner that loudly proclaimed Down With the Monarchy. Seeing it was a shock.

So, she thought, *this is not quite the paradise the king wants me to believe it is.*

It took her a moment to realize that Madeline was at her elbow. "Didn't realize you were an actress," her friend whispered to her, barely moving her lips.

"Every princess is," Amelia responded in the same low whisper. The smile she'd summoned remained on her lips as she looked out on the crowd. Turning toward the king, she nodded toward the small cluster of dissenters. "Who are they?"

"No one you need concern yourself about," Weston replied dismissively.

"That's the Union for Democracy," Russell told her. "Nikolas Donovan is their leader. He would be the one you see in front."

All she could see was Russell. But she was a princess and knew she had to conduct herself as one—as if nothing was crossing her mind but the information he was telling her, as if her pulse was not accelerating, even now. "Are they dangerous?" she wanted to know.

"Peaceful," he countered.

She nodded. "I hope they stay that way."

"I won't have them ruining this occasion," the king told her firmly. He extended his arm to her. "If you'll permit me, Princess?"

Amelia slipped her arm through his. "Of course." As he led her to the long, sleek, black limousine that was to take them back to the palace, she inclined her head toward his and asked the question she could no longer keep back. "Where is the prince?"

She felt the king stiffen, saw the smile on his lips grow just a little brittle around the edges. Clearly this was a sore point. And then she understood that by not being here, Reginald was not only insulting her, but the king, as well. He paused as they came to the limousine. "No one knows."

The driver hurriedly opened the door for them, then stood back.

"I see," she murmured, slipping into the limousine first.

The king followed, taking his seat beside her. By rights, Russell should have come next, but he stepped back, gesturing for Madeline to get into the vehicle before him. Madeline gave him a wide, appreciative grin before ducking her head and taking the seat opposite Amelia.

Manners before protocol, Amelia thought. In her heart, she knew that it would have never occurred to Reginald to surrender his position and allow Madeline to get into the vehicle before him. She could hear his young voice taunting her.

When we're grown, you'll have to mind me and do everything I say. You won't have a choice.

He'd been a dictator even then. Was he one now? Was she going to find life with him unbearable? She strove not to let depression absorb her thoughts, strove not to think beyond the moment. She should be relieved, not insulted, by Reginald's absence, she told herself.

The king's bodyguard closed the door and the vehicle began its journey to the palace, less than five miles away.

Progress was slow. People lined both sides of the streets, waving frantically even before the limousine passed them. Some held tiny Silvershire flags. A few clutched both the flags of Silvershire and Gastonia, symbolizing the merger of the two kingdoms. The mood was festive.

Everywhere but within the interior of the limousine.

Amelia sat closest to the window, waving to the faces of her new people. Though she tried not to focus on it, the significance of the prince's continued and very glaring absence from the scene weighed down on her.

This didn't bode well for the marriage, she thought, her smile never faltering. But then, she had already sensed that. Otherwise, she would have never invited Russell to her bed, no matter how drawn to him she felt.

Hers was not destined to be a fairy-tale marriage, Amelia reflected sadly, struggling to accept what she knew was her fate. Still, she continued waving and smiling at the people who wished her well and who were already, from all appearances, taking her to their hearts.

All except for the small band of dissenters.

Chapter 7

Discreet questions as to the prince's whereabouts were asked once the limousine arrived at the palace. But no one seemed to know where Reginald was. The king's anxiety continued to mount even as he prepared to attend the gala being held at the palace in honor of Princess Amelia's arrival and the young royals' upcoming wedding.

The hours slipped by. The prince was nowhere to be found.

Russell frowned to himself, returning his cell phone to his pocket. Reginald wasn't answering his personal phone. Voice mail picked up immediately, which meant that the prince had shut off his phone, something he was prone to doing whenever he was busy gratifying his sexual appetites. Dutifully, Russell informed the king that his son couldn't be reached.

On the advice of his chief counselor, King Weston changed the theme of the celebration at the last moment to center exclusively around the princess who had come to join together the two kingdoms.

Outwardly, the mood at the party was festive, but beneath the thin layer of gaiety was an underlying knot of tension. Because they cared for their king and had taken to the princess, everyone at the affair pretended that there was nothing wrong.

As he stood back and observed the guests, Russell was convinced that the prince's glaring absence was the talk of every small gathering he saw at the celebration.

At least Amelia was a hit, Russell thought fondly. But then, how could she not be? Coddling the scotch and soda he had been nursing for the last half hour, Russell smiled to himself. The change in Princess Amelia had been incredible. It was hard to believe that this was the same young girl who'd been the target of his practical jokes whenever he'd visited Gastonia.

Taking a sip from his glass, he felt the liquid spread a deep, burning sensation through his chest, warming everything in its path. It was the same sort of sensation he experienced each time he now looked in Amelia's direction.

All evening, Amelia continued to be the center of attention. At the moment Russell watched her engage several of Silvershire's leading businessmen in conversation. The perfunctory smiles on the men's faces quickly changed to looks of interest. Russell knew for a fact that the princess, in addition to being fluent in five different languages, had a business degree to her name.

The five languages put her four and a half up on Reginald, he thought with a touch of cynicism.

It seemed that there was nothing, Russell thought with more than a little pride, she couldn't accomplish if she set her mind to it.

She was charming the pants off everyone, Russell noted. God knew that she had certainly done that with him. Even before they had spent the night together.

He felt a pang stirring within him, born not of guilt but of need. It was followed by a wave of anger. The prince should be horsewhipped for standing her up this way. Reginald had known about this gala, known that it was to have celebrated their upcoming marriage. How could he *do* this to Amelia?

The very thought of the marriage, of Amelia being intimate with Reginald, made something in the pit of his stomach rise up in his throat. Russell took another sip to wash the taste of bile from his mouth.

He had no business feeling like this, no business feeling anything beyond a mild pity for whoever officially graced the prince's bed. But he couldn't help himself. This was personal. It would always be personal no matter how much he wanted to divorce himself from the situation. He realized that his hand was tightening around his glass and he forced himself to relax his grip.

Were this another time, one of intrigue and secret pacts, when daggers rather than words were used to settle matters of discord, he might have been sorely tempted...

To what? To kill Reginald?

No, Russell thought, murder wasn't his way. And it

certainly wasn't an option, even if he were the kind of person who thought nothing of killing whoever got in his way. It wasn't an option because Russell had always prided himself on his loyalty to the crown, and Reginald was the future king of Silvershire.

Which meant that he had to be loyal to Reginald, no matter what. Even though, despite all of his and the king's efforts, Reginald would undoubtedly turn out to be a bad king. But whether Reginald was or not, it was not a matter for him to take into his own hands.

Just as he shouldn't have taken Amelia into his hands, into his arms, Russell thought. That he had was his cross to bear. In silence.

He figured the almost bottomless longing he felt would make him pay for his transgression every day of his life. Even now, watching the princess as groups of men and women gathered around her, he felt himself wanting her more than he could recall ever wanting anyone before.

Hell of a cross to bear, he thought darkly, taking another drink.

"So where do you suppose he really is?"

The question came out of nowhere, as if echoing his thoughts. Glancing to his side, he saw Amelia's lady-in-waiting, Madeline. He'd been so lost in his thoughts and in observing Amelia from what he'd initially thought was a safe distance—quickly learning that there was no safe distance when it came to being around Amelia—that he hadn't heard the princess's friend approach.

From the little he had seen of her, Madeline struck him as being very honest and straightforward. By no stretch of the imagination could the lady be called shy or retiring. She was outspoken and seemed a perfect match for Amelia.

For the princess, he upbraided himself. He had to stop thinking of her by her given name and just keep reminding himself that she was the princess. And would be, in a matter of weeks, his queen. Continuing to regard her as Amelia was out of order.

He inclined his head toward Madeline, pretending he hadn't heard her. "Excuse me?"

Madeline gave him a look that said she knew that he knew what she was talking about. But for form's sake, she elaborated.

"The prince," she enunciated precisely, wishing she could grind the man between her teeth, as well. "Why isn't he here?"

Russell paused. Protocol dictated that he say something in the man's defense. That he tell this woman of less-than-royal blood that it wasn't any of her concern what the prince did, or didn't do, or where he was at any given moment. But he was far too modern in his thinking for that. And he liked the fact that Amelia had a friend to help her at a time like this. A friend who could be open.

You're her friend. Except that, because of what had happened between them, he couldn't allow himself to assume that role any longer. People would talk. He wanted nothing to sully her reputation. Nothing.

This was a very sticky situation they found themselves in, he thought ruefully.

"I don't know," he told Madeline honestly. And then,

because he felt he could trust the young woman, he added, "This behavior is pretty reckless, even for the prince."

Madeline had put her own interpretation to the prince's no-show. Or maybe it was just wishful thinking on her part. "Is this his way of saying that he won't go through with the marriage?"

That had never been in jeopardy, Russell thought sadly. "Oh, the prince'll go through with the marriage. There's too much riding on it for him not to. He might be reckless, but he's not brave enough to oppose his father in matters that really count."

Madeline frowned, taking offense for Amelia who was too kind-hearted to voice her own offense. "And not coming here doesn't count?" she wanted to know. "You know, someone other than Princess Amelia would have been humiliated."

"She's made of finer stuff than that," Russell commented, looking in Amelia's direction again.

Unintentionally, he caught Amelia's eye. For a moment, they looked at one another from across the room and he could almost feel a communion between them. But it wasn't anything that either one of them could acknowledge, even fleetingly, without consequences.

He looked away first, before anyone could see. Or so he thought.

"Yes," Madeline agreed, noting what had just happened between the duke and Amelia, even if everyone else was oblivious to it, "she is." Moving closer to Carrington, she lowered her voice. "Maybe the princess is also lucky. Maybe the prince will find that backbone every living creature is supposed to have and use it to sail away to Tahiti." She flashed a smile at him. "At least, one can hope." She ended her statement with a wink, then excused herself before drifting back over toward Amelia.

The princess's lady had winked at him. Was that supposed to mean something? Was she flirting with him, or delivering some kind of a message?

God, but he did hate complications.

Turning away to refill the drink he had finally finished, Russell all but walked into a solid wall of a man. One of the king's six bodyguards. This one was a tall, burly man who looked as uncomfortable in the tuxedo he was forced to wear as he would have been in a ballet dress fashioned with a profusion of tulle.

He gave a perfunctory nod of his head in place of a bow. "Excuse me, Your Grace, but King Weston would like to speak with you."

"The king?" Russell looked around and saw that Weston was not anywhere in the ballroom. If the royals continued to disappear like this, he mused, Nikolas Donovan and his Union for Democracy would find that winning their battle took no effort at all.

"Yes. This way, please."

They left the ballroom. Russell followed the bodyguard into the corridor and then to the king's study.

"Here he is, Your Majesty," the bodyguard announced. The moment that Russell crossed the threshold, the other man closed the doors behind him. Russell had no doubt that the man had positioned himself outside the double doors, barring anyone else's entrance until the king was finished with him.

Alone, with no prying eyes to spy on him, King Weston allowed his smiling facade to fall away. He'd known Russell since the young duke and Reginald had played together in a royal, pristine white sandbox. He felt comfortable enough with Russell not to have to maintain a pose. The man was almost like his own son.

In some ways, he actually felt *more* comfortable in Russell's presence than in Reginald's. There was an honesty to Russell that was missing in his own son.

His frown went deep, almost clear down to the bone. As did his frustration and displeasure. "Where the hell is he, Russell?"

"I don't know." He was surprised to see that the king fixed him with a long, hard, penetrating look. "I would tell you, Your Majesty, if I knew." He watched as the expression faded from Weston's face. "But I've been gone these last few days," he reminded his ruler, "bringing the princess back for the wedding."

"The wedding." Despair almost got the better of Weston as he threw up his hands.

Of late, the King had been battling the effects of what he took to be the flu. He felt feverish, at times dizzy, although he said nothing because he did not want the royal doctor fussing over him. But feeling the way he did, he was not up to Reginald's latest display of inexcusable behavior.

"The wedding is taking place in three days. No, two and a half," he amended. "Two and a half days," he repeated.

Russell truly felt sorry for what he thought the king had to be going through. Every man wanted to point to his son with pride, not frustration. "I know that, Your Majesty," he responded quietly.

"What if he decides to skip that, too, just like he skipped meeting her at the airport, just like he skipped attending the party in his and her honor?" The tension in the king's voice kept building, fueled by ever-increasing agitation. "What if he doesn't come? What am I to do then, marry the girl off to a piece of his clothing? Or to the royal sword?"

Though the situation was deadly serious, the question threatened to evoke a smile. Russell did his best to keep it at bay.

"Marriage by proxy has been done, Your Majesty," Russell allowed.

"Yes, it has. During the Crusades," the king retorted angrily. "What is he thinking?" The question was more of a lament than a demand for an answer.

Russell had been with the prince on more than one of his escapades and knew the pattern of Reginald's behavior as the evening advanced. "Right about now, Your Majesty, since the prince is missing, I don't imagine that he's thinking much of anything."

Weston's pale complexion took on color. "Because he's dead drunk?"

Russell deliberately kept his voice low, hoping to calm the king down. "That, too, I'm afraid, has been known to happen."

The king shook his head, not in despair, but in final decision. He had indulged Reginald too long and too much. He had to put a stop to it and he would. Beginning now. The prince couldn't be allowed to continue behaving like some rutting stag.

"Well, it can't," the king said with finality.. "Not

anymore. He has to learn that he has to grow up. Reginald's thirty years old, for heaven's sake."

The king had begun to pace. Russell moved out of the way, giving the monarch a clear path. "Yes, I know that, too, Your Majesty."

Weston paused abruptly, as if to gather himself together. His complexion, Russell thought, was much too red. If the king was not careful, he could talk himself right into a heart attack or a stroke. He'd heard rumors, although as of yet unsubstantiated, that the king's health was not what it used to be. No doubt, Reginald and his reckless behavior had something to do with that.

The king crossed to him. They were of equal height. The king looked at him imploringly, not as a ruler but as a father. A father who had been pushed to the limit of his endurance. "I want you to find him for me, Russell."

Russell didn't want to make promises he couldn't keep. "I don't—"

The king held up his hand, not letting him finish. "You know his haunts, you know what he's capable of and with whom." A sad smile curved her lips. "Probably much more than I do. I pride myself on being informed, but there are some things a father doesn't want to know about his son." His eyes met Russell's in a silent entreaty for understanding. "So I have no idea where to send one of my bodyguards to find him. But you would know." He paused, waiting for some kind of confirmation. "Wouldn't you?"

Even though he didn't go there himself, he knew the different places that Reginald liked to frequent, some he wouldn't even repeat to the king. "There are a few places I could go to look."

"Then go. Look." The words came out like shots fired from a gun, quick, independent and lethal. "And bring the prince back, even if he orders you not to." Weston squared his broad shoulders. "You have my orders and I can still overrule the prince."

But for how long? Russell wondered. Once Weston gave up the crown to his son, Russell had more than just an uneasy feeling that there would be no safeguards that could be applied to the unruly Reginald. There would be no one to stop him, at least, not officially. Russell foresaw only turmoil in the months ahead. The way he felt about Amelia had nothing to do with his fears for the realm.

He studied his monarch's face. The king was an intelligent man. Granted he loved his son, but he had to see that Reginald wasn't really fit to take charge, no matter what his chronological age. They needed more time to make him ready to assume his responsibilities. Until now, Reginald had only been playing at being a royal. He had taken on none of the duties that went with his position.

For heaven's sake, he couldn't even show up somewhere on time.

The words burned on his tongue. Russell couldn't allow himself just to stand by and say nothing. But he knew the path was one that was lined with mines. He picked his way carefully.

"Perhaps, Your Majesty, you might reconsider the coronation ceremony," Russell suggested tactfully. "Postpone the official shift of power for a little while until such time as—"

The king wouldn't let him finish. He raised his hand, stopping Russell. "I understand what you are saying, Carrington, and believe me, I have had the same thoughts. More than once," he added heavily. "But I can't go against tradition. I can't simply break rules when it suits me and expect others not to."

Russell knew that by "others" the king was referring to the troublesome Union for Democracy. There had been efforts, ever since the group had organized five years ago, to suppress it, to try as subtly as possible to force the members to disband. But instead, it had only grown. Not by any large degree, but enough to deserve further close surveillance. They called themselves a peaceful group, but more than one so-called peaceful group had been known to become the center of violent eruptions. No one wanted to see that happen in Silvershire.

Russell found himself wondering if perhaps having the Union of Democracy take over might not, in the final analysis, be preferable to having Reginald ascend to the throne.

But he kept this to himself as he inclined his head, symbolizing his acquiescing to his ruler's wishes. "Yes, Your Majesty."

"Go find my son and tell him…tell him…" It was on the tip of Weston's tongue to instruct Russell to say to Reginald that he was a disappointment to him. But that was between him and his son. No one else, not even Russell, as familiar as he was with the scene, was allowed to be privy to that. "Just tell the prince to hurry back to the palace and live up to his responsibilities," he concluded.

"Yes, Your Majesty." Russell paused, reading between the lines. The gala was still going on, but he had no real desire to remain. He would rather be busy than standing around, left to his own thoughts. Thoughts he found difficult to deal with at the moment. "Do you want me to go this evening?"

"Yes, if you would. Now," Weston emphasized. And then he confided, "I have this dreadful feeling that every moment matters."

Russell thought of telling the king that he had no need to worry. That Reginald was just being Reginald, shallow and thoughtless and self-involved. That he was most likely in some estate, sleeping off a drinking spree, or availing himself of any one of a number of willing women who wanted to be able to boast to their friends that they had slept with an authentic prince.

But in the end, he decided that perhaps discretion was the better road to take. So he bowed and withdrew. "Yes, Your Majesty."

Russell sighed, relieved to have an excuse to go home and change out of the tuxedo that fit him like a dark glove. He didn't care that he looked good in it, it was stiff and uncomfortable. He'd never liked formal attire. His rank in life called for it, so he put up with it when it was called for, but he was far happier wearing jeans and a sweater. He had the soul of a commoner, his father used to chide him. He suspected that his father was right.

As he turned the corner on his way out of the palace, he almost walked directly into Amelia. The unexpected contact was quick and sharp, as were the pins and needles that shot all through his body.

Without thinking, he'd reached to grab for her, to steady her in case she was going to fall. Reflexes had him doing it even before he realized who it was that he had bumped into, although his body immediately recognized the familiar feel of the impact. All it took, he thought, was once, and the feel of her body had been indelibly pressed onto the pages of his memory.

God, but he was waxing poetic. At another time, it would have been enough to turn his own stomach. Was this what love did to you? Turned you into someone you wouldn't normally associate with if you had a choice? He had no answer to that. No answer to anything, except that he was being turned inside out.

Did it get better with time? He could only fervently hope so.

But something told him that he was hoping in vain.

Attempting to collect himself, he retreated to the shelter of formal decorum and released Amelia.

"I'm sorry, I shouldn't have grabbed you like that, but I was afraid you'd fall. Are you lost, Princess?" He congratulated himself on his formal tone. One never knew who might be listening in the palace and he wanted no hint of a stain upon her reputation.

She raised her eyes to his. "Yes," she answered quietly, "I'm afraid I am lost." After a beat, she added, "Very lost."

As her eyes held his, Russell knew she wasn't talking about finding her way through the palace.

Chapter 8

He was a man who prided himself on remaining cool under fire. And although standing in the hallway with the Princess of Gastonia could hardly be designated as being under fire, Russell felt himself growing more than a little warm.

As was she, he thought. Her cheeks were flushed and the temperature within the palace was moderate at best. The king liked it brisk. He maintained that it got the blood moving.

His blood, Russell thought, was having no trouble moving. Close proximity to the Princess Amelia had seen to that.

He realized that several seconds had passed and he hadn't responded to her words yet. His brain felt as if it had been taken hostage. It took effort and concentration in order to free it.

"It's a little overwhelming until you get used to it," Russell finally managed. "The palace," he added in case the princess misunderstood his meaning.

Damn, he sounded like some thick-tongued fool. He'd never possessed Reginald's silver tongue, but he'd never been a babbling idiot, either. Not until now.

But then, he'd never slept with a princess before. That changed things.

He had to put that behind him, Russell insisted silently. And what's more, they couldn't just stand in the corridor, exchanging nonsense like this. There was no telling who might see them and misconstrue things.

Or construe them correctly, he thought ruefully.

The lighting in the corridor was sufficiently bright, yet it paled in comparison to her, he thought. Everything paled in comparison to her.

He felt the long, slender fingers of temptation reaching for him. Threatening to ensnare him again. He couldn't pretend that he didn't want her; he did. All he could do was struggle for control.

But a man's control only went so far and not nearly enough time had gone by for the embers of the fire that had been lit between them to have cooled.

Not enough time had gone by for him to have cooled, either.

Just looking at her made him long for a different place, a different time. A different life.

"I just wanted to get a little air." She touched his arm as she spoke and he could literally feel the heat flaring through him. He did his best to bank it down and ignore it.

"There isn't much to be had in the corridor," he pointed out with amusement.

"More than there is in there." She nodded in the general direction of the ballroom she had just left. "Too many questions, too many people," she explained and then looked up at him. "Too many doubts."

He tried to focus on something other than her lips. On something other than the way he wanted to taste them again. "Princess—"

Second-guessing his response, she held up her hand to stop him.

"Oh, I know what my duty is," she said quickly and with resignation. "I've known what my duty was since before I could adequately understand what the word itself really meant. But the doubts I have are about the prince himself. He seems neither to know, nor to care what his obligations are as far as maintaining at least a civil relationship with his future wife." She pressed her lips together, digging deep for courage and resolve in order to get through this. "I'm not sure I can face marriage to a man who has so little regard for me that he does not even attend a ceremony meant to welcome me to his kingdom. A ceremony meant to honor us as a royal couple."

Were those tears he saw in her eyes? God, he hoped not. He had no idea what to do when faced with a woman's tears. He would much rather have spent an entire day arguing with the prince than five seconds in the company of a tearful woman.

All the more so because he was left with the odious job of having to defend the errant royal. "I'm sure he was unavoidably detained."

To his surprise, Amelia laughed shortly. "Hand-cuffed to a bed?"

Only supreme control kept his jaw from dropping. "Princess—"

And then she laughed, really laughed. That light, airy sound that had already won a place in his heart. The same heart that had pledged its loyalty to the crown, to the prince. He felt guilty as hell and torn in two diametrically opposed directions.

"Don't look so shocked, Carrington. I wasn't raised in an eighteenth-century cloister." She lowered her voice and seemed to draw closer, even though she didn't move a muscle. "You, more than anyone, should know that."

Was that the sound of approaching footsteps he heard? Russell looked around. He had no thought about himself, but there was the princess's honor to be concerned about. "We really shouldn't be seen talking like this—" he began to warn her.

A smattering of impatience crossed her brow. It occurred to him that Amelia was undoubtedly one of those types who looked magnificent when she was angry.

"Who shall I talk to? Madeline seems to have been charmed out of her shoes by one of the young dukes and the king is not exactly the person I can turn to with concerns about his son. The poor man looks put upon enough without having to listen to me voice my misgivings. Besides," she confided, "I haven't seen the king in more than half an hour."

"That's because he's in his study." He indicated the area just beyond the corner. "I just came from there. His Majesty requested that I find and bring back the prince." Russell saw an odd expression filter across her face. He was unable to fathom it. Had he said something wrong? "What is it?"

This, Amelia thought, had to be the definition of irony. "I find myself in a very precarious position. I don't know whether to hope that you do find him, or hope that you don't. For me, it seems to be the epitome of a lose-lose situation." But, because she was a princess and raised by her father to put her country before her own needs, Amelia rallied and then offered Russell a smile. "Of course I hope you find him. One should never misplace a prince. It's bad for the country."

As well Reginald might be, Russell couldn't help thinking. He really wished that Weston could continue as king for years to come.

And then Amelia stepped back, as if to re-enter the ballroom. "I shouldn't be detaining you, Carrington. Good luck."

The way she'd said it, he wasn't quite sure if she meant with his assignment, or something else. "With finding the prince?"

"With whatever it is you want to happen," she corrected.

With that, Amelia turned on her heel and returned to the ballroom and to the mountain of responsibilities that were waiting for her just inside the door.

* * *

It was the last place Russell would have thought to look. It was the last place he did look, because it had seemed so improbable. So tame.

For the last twelve hours, Russell had gone from one club to another, methodically working his way from the more prestigious ones down to the clubs that no one willingly admitted, at least in public, that they frequented. The ones for which the phrase *den of iniquity* had originally been fashioned.

But no matter where he went, the story always seemed to be the same. Yes, the prince had been there, but no one had seen the prince within the last two days. When he questioned the men who were often with the prince about his whereabouts, they all claimed to believe that he was at some other place, with another set of cohorts.

Russell had to bank down the intense desire to shout at the men to sober up and do something meaningful with their lives. But that, he knew, was merely displacement. The words were meant for the prince.

Russell shook his head as he left the last establishment. At the prince's present pace, Reginald would probably wind up bedding or at least propositioning every woman in Silvershire under the age of eighty by summer's end.

He got back behind the wheel of his vehicle and slammed the door. Funny, he hadn't realized how much he loathed the man until this very moment. Even animals in the wild were more monogamous than Reginald was, and he wasn't even thinking of the ones who mated for life. Reginald mated for an hour, then went on, amnesia clouding his brain.

And this was going to be their future ruler.

God had to have one hell of a sense of humor, Russell thought darkly, starting the car again.

He was out of places. Out of glitzy clubs and run-down holes-in-the-wall. He'd already checked with the airports and the harbor. The prince had not left the country by means public or private. Since Silvershire was seabound on all sides, that meant that he was here.

But where?

Deciding that when he reported to the king, he wanted to have been utterly thorough, Russell could only think of one more place to try. A place where he was fairly certain the prince wasn't: his country estate. The king had given him the deed to the property on his twenty-first birthday. When the novelty of owning a country estate had still been fresh, Reginald had thrown there more than a few of what could only be politely referred to as orgies.

He himself had begun drawing the line then, Russell recalled. The very thought of what went on there turned his stomach. But Reginald seemed to thrive on those decadent gatherings. The more participants, the better.

Angry for the princess, for the country, Russell's mood was black by the time he reached the estate.

As he'd expected, there was no one there. The only time there was any staff at the estate, aside from the gardener who was dispatched once a month and the housekeeper who cleaned on a weekly basis, was when the prince was in residence there.

He recalled that, just before he'd left for Gastonia,

Reginald had told him that he would be visiting the estate. He'd thought Reginald was joking, but this was no time to leave any stone unturned.

The estate was shrouded in silence as the last rays of late-afternoon light receded. Russell disarmed the alarm and unlocked the front door. The prince had entrusted him with the code and a key to the estate as a token of their friendship.

A friendship, Russell thought as he closed the door behind him, that had long since lost its luster—if it had ever had any to begin with.

The house absorbed darkness with the thirst of a sponge. Russell turned on the light that illuminated the foyer and hallway beyond.

"Hello, is anyone here?"

His voice echoed back, mocking him as he crossed the marble foyer. The heels of his shoes meeting the stone was the only sound he heard.

This was useless. The Black Prince was probably holed up in some woman's bedroom, waiting for his fourth or fifth wind. When it came to making love, Reginald was tireless. Too bad he wasn't like that when it came to matters of state.

Russell paused, debating going back to the palace. And then he shrugged. He was here. He might as well check the bedrooms and the kitchen. That way, he could tell the king that he had looked everywhere he could possibly think of for the prince.

"Why don't you just grow up, Reginald?" Russell said out loud in exasperation. "The princess is a beautiful woman. She'll make you happy. And you, you should drop down on your knees and thank God that you, with your black soul, were still lucky enough to get such a woman."

On the second floor, Russell marched up and down the hall, pushing open one door after another as he spoke, venting his frustration. "Your father's right. It's time for you to grow up and be a man for once in your life, not just some—"

The words caught in Russell's throat.

The bedroom wasn't empty. There was someone in the bed.

He hadn't really expected to find the prince. At best this was just an exercise in futility to cover all the bases. But there he was, in bed, stark naked from all appearances, with a sheet draped over his loins, and sound asleep as if he didn't have a care in the world.

"Damn it, Reginald," he said in the familiar voice of a man who had been a friend for more years than he should have, "how can you just lie there like that? Don't you know that everyone's been waiting for you to turn up for the last two days? You didn't come to the airport, you didn't come to the gala. You're supposed to be getting married in two days. How can you be—"

Exasperated, Russell abruptly halted what he felt was a well-deserved tirade. The prince was sleeping through it all, anyway.

With a weary sigh, Russell crossed to the bed and took hold of the prince's shoulder, shaking it. Reginald was a sounder sleeper than most, especially when he'd been drinking, so Russell shook him again. There was still no response, no indication that the prince was waking up. His expression remained unchanged.

"Sleeping the sleep of the dead?" Russell mocked with no trace of humor. "Because it certainly isn't the sleep of the just. Well, I don't care how drunk you are, the king sent me to find you and find you I did, so come on, get up. Get up and get dressed, your father's waiting. You've really done it this time with those 'wild oats' of yours and it's going to take a lot to reverse all the bad press you've been getting."

The prince remained inert.

Russell looked at him. Something wasn't right.

He could feel it in his bones. Feel it just the way he had when he had been away at school and had suddenly sensed that his father had fallen ill. That his father needed him. He had no idea how he'd known, he just had. He'd come home just in time to be at his side when his father had died.

A gut feeling had prompted him then. And now he was experiencing another one.

Russell dropped down to one knee beside the bed, staring at the prince. "Reginald?"

The prince's hand felt cold when he took it. The sensation registered the very same moment that he realized the prince's chest wasn't moving. Reginald wasn't breathing.

Adrenaline raced through his veins as Russell tried to find a pulse. There was none. As he looked more closely at the prince, he had the sickening feeling that there hadn't been a pulse for at least several hours.

Perhaps even a day. The body was not stiff, but rigor mortis was a condition that came and then receded.

He needed an expert. He needed help.

"Oh, God," Russell groaned under his breath. Rising to his feet, he took out his cell phone and quickly called the royal physician. The number was on his speed dial. The man had been summoned on a fairly regular basis for more than a decade, always to see to the prince after a lengthy spate of debauchery.

"What's the matter?" There was a hint of irritation in the doctor's voice once Russell had identified himself. "Is he hungover again?"

Russell glanced over his shoulder at the still form. "I'm afraid he's much more than that, Doctor." Rather than ask the doctor to come, he told the man what was wrong. "The prince is dead."

"Dead?" the doctor echoed in a hushed voice throbbing with disbelief. Everyone associated with Reginald had come to believe that he had a charmed life. "How did it happen?"

Russell leaned over the body. There were no telltale marks to identify the cause.

"I have no idea. He wasn't shot or stabbed and doesn't look to have been strangled. Everything is neat and as far as I can tell, in its place. There's no evidence of any kind of a struggle." These days, with the preponderance of television crime programs that came to them thanks to the Americans, everyone was an armchair crime-scene investigator, Russell thought, and that included him.

"We're going to need an autopsy." He heard rustling

on the other end. The doctor was preparing to leave. "Does the king know?"

"Not yet." There was a reason why he had delayed that call. He was afraid of what the shock of Reginald's death might do to the king. "I wanted to give you some time to reach him before I called. He's probably going to need to be sedated."

The doctor's tone indicated that he was not so sure. "Don't underestimate the old man. He's a lot tougher than you think."

"Even tough men have been known to fall apart and he hasn't been looking too good lately," Russell said quietly. "How long will it take you to get to the palace?"

The doctor didn't need any time to consider. He'd made the trip often enough, both from his home and from his office. "Fifteen minutes."

"All right. I'll wait fifteen minutes, then," Russell replied. "Once you see to the king, I need you to come here."

"Of course," the man agreed. "And here would be—?"

"The prince's country estate."

"I'm on my way," the doctor promised.

His eyes never leaving the prince's body, Russell slowly closed his cell phone and slipped it back into his pocket. A shaft of guilt pierced him. God help him, but his first thought was that Amelia wasn't going to have to go through with the wedding.

He couldn't think about that now.

There was a brocade armchair in the corner of the room beside the window. Russell dragged it over next to the bed and then lowered himself into it, his eyes never leaving Reginald's body.

What a waste. What a terrible waste.

He thought for a moment of dressing the prince, of giving him a dignity in death that Reginald had turned his back on while he'd been alive. But he knew better than to tamper with anything. Although there were indications that the prince might just have finally taken the wrong combination of alcohol and drugs, this might still be considered a crime scene. It was bad enough that he had touched first Reginald's shoulder and then the pulse at both the prince's throat and his wrist. He didn't want to compromise the scene any further.

Russell folded his hands in his lap and proceeded to wait for the longest fifteen minutes of his life. The minute hand on the ancient timepiece his grandfather had given him dragged by like a snail dipped in molasses working its way along a rough surface. It seemed almost frozen in place each time he looked at it.

Fifteen minutes took forever. But finally, the minute hand touched the sixteenth stroke. Russell flipped his cell phone open once again and called the palace.

It took several more minutes for someone find the king. He'd initially met with resistance when he refused to divulge the reason behind his call, saying only that the king was expecting it.

No father ever expected this kind of a call, Russell thought sadly.

As modern-thinking as the king was, Weston refused to carry a cell phone, feeling that it was too invasive.

When he finally came on the telephone to speak to him, Weston was on one of the palace's secured land lines.

"This is King Weston," the deep, unmistakable baritone voice echoed against his ear.

God, I wish I didn't have to tell you this. "Your Majesty, it's Carrington."

The king's voice was immediately eager. "Did you find him? Did you find the prince?"

Each word felt like molten lead as it left his tongue. "Yes, Your Majesty, I did, but—"

"What did he have to say for himself?" the monarch demanded. It was obvious that although he had been indulgent for all of Reginald's life, the king was finally coming to the end of his patience.

"Nothing." Russell stalled for a moment, still concerned about the king's health despite what the doctor had said. "Your Majesty, is the royal physician with you yet?"

"No, why should he—" There was a pause. Russell heard the sound of someone knocking and then a door being opened in the background. "Doctor, what are you doing here? Is someone ill?" the king asked, addressing the doctor.

"No, Your Majesty," Russell answered for the physician. "The doctor is there to help you."

"Help me?" the king echoed, confused. "Why would I need a doctor—?" Abruptly, a note of fear entered his voice. "Carrington, there's something wrong, isn't there?"

"I'm afraid there is, Your Majesty."

Russell could almost hear the king holding his breath. As if by not breathing, that would forestall whatever bad news was coming. "It's Reginald, isn't it?"

"Yes, Your Majesty, it is." It was as if the words refused to materialize, refuse to enter the atmosphere.

There was desperation in the king's voice. He was stalling, trying to find a reason for this melodrama that he could live with. "What kind of trouble has he gotten himself into this time?"

There was no way to say this, no way to couch the words that had to come out so that they wouldn't leave wounds, wouldn't hurt beyond measure. In his heart, Russell damned the prince for living the kind of lifestyle that had brought him to this. Most of all, he damned Reginald for making him have to say this to the king.

"Your Majesty, Prince Reginald is dead."

"No," the king cried. "No! This is a lie, a trick. You're not telling me the truth. Reginald is trying to play me, the way he always has before. So, what does he want? What does he hope to gain from all this?"

"Nothing, Your Majesty. This isn't a hoax. I'm very sorry to be the one to have to tell you this, but the prince really is dead. I found him at his country estate and he's been dead for hours, perhaps more."

He heard the receiver being dropped. And then the line on the other end went dead.

Chapter 9

Russell folded his cell phone and placed it back into his pocket. He didn't try to reach the king again. He knew that they hadn't been disconnected because of any signal that failed to get through. Undoubtedly, the king had terminated the conversation, unable to listen any longer. He couldn't blame him. He had no idea how he would have reacted in the monarch's place.

But then, he would have kept a tighter rein on Reginald than the king ever had. Maybe if safeguards had been put into place early on, if rules and a sense of moral values had been drummed into the prince's head, he wouldn't be where he was right now.

Naked and alone.

Well, almost alone, Russell amended. He shook his head, looking down at the cause of the king's grief.

"Well, you did it again, Reggie. Even in death, you've managed to disrupt everyone else's life."

And even in death, the prince had managed to be selfish, without a care for those he left behind.

Russell was worried about the king. Granted, to the passing observer, except for the last few days, the king looked to be in excellent condition, especially considering his age, but that was just the outside packaging. He knew, though it was never publicized, that the king had a number of health issues, none of them ever elaborated on, which, of course, was understandable. The public wanted an invincible ruler. If the king had a heart condition, or some sort of other malady, that would be a matter only between the king and his doctor. No one else would ever need know.

The king was by nature a private man. It physically upset him that Reginald brought so much attention to his less-than-sterling behavior. The escapades of the last few weeks had taken a toll on the monarch. His color had paled and he looked…unwell, Russell supposed was the best term for it. News of Reginald's death might cause his health to take a sudden downward spiral.

Sharp nettles of regret dragged along his conscience. Maybe he should have waited before calling the king, or better yet, left the job of breaking the news to the royal physician.

But that would have been cowardly, he upbraided himself, and he was not a coward. He did what needed to be done, regardless of the personal consequences. In all good conscience, the king had to be informed and the sooner the better. Russell knew the king. If Weston learned that he had been kept in the dark, even for his own good, he would not take the news well.

No, he'd acted accordingly, Russell decided as late-afternoon shadows began to take possession of the room. The misgivings he was having were rooted in the guilt he still felt over sleeping with the princess. In a single reckless act, he had betrayed the king, the prince, his country and his own set of values. The passage of time was not going to change the way he felt about that.

He doubted if he would ever be right with his actions, no matter how much he cared for the princess. It was something a man of honor should not have done. Despite the reasons, there was no excuse for it.

With a heavy sigh, Russell sat back in the chair, keeping vigil.

The royal physician arrived with an ambulance forty-five minutes later. To stay under the radar and not attract any unwanted attention until the matter of the prince was properly attended to, there were no sirens, no telltale indication that there was any urgency. Still, Russell had a feeling that the driver had bent all the speed limits to get to the estate in the amount of time that he had.

Russell went outside to meet the vehicle and was surprised to see a very shaken-looking King Weston emerge from the rear of the ambulance. He almost looked fragile, Russell thought. The monarch was accompanied only by the ambulance driver, the royal physician and his chief bodyguard, Bostwick, who had been with the king since he had first accepted the crown, thirty years ago.

Weston was as pale as a ghost. Russell learned later from the doctor that the king had collapsed when he'd heard that Reginald was dead and had had to be revived. But nothing would convince him not to come with the ambulance to tend to his son.

"Where is he?" Weston demanded hoarsely, striding past Russell and walking into the mansion. His voice echoed within the vaulted ceilings. "Where is my son?"

"This way, Your Majesty." Russell moved around the monarch and led him up the stairs to the bedroom where he'd found the prince.

Grimly, he stood to the side of the doorway, allowing the king to enter first. The monarch seemed to be in almost a trance as he crossed to the bed and stood over his only son.

Dr. Neubert walked in behind him. In his service for only a few years, the young physician was concerned about the toll this was having on his monarch's heart and general health.

"Your Majesty, you shouldn't—" Dr. Neubert began.

Weston waved him into silence with an impatient gesture.

From his vantage point, Russell could see the tears gathering in the king's blue-gray eyes. Protocol dictated that he hang back, that he allow the king his dignity, his moment, but Russell thought of him as a second father and as such, could not bring himself to leave the man standing so alone. He crossed to stand beside him.

"I've lived too long, Russell," the king finally said, his eyes never leaving the inert form. "No father should have to see his son dead before him." He swayed slightly and Russell was quick to lend his support, steadying him. That Weston was in a bad way became imminently clear when the king did not shrug him away but accepted his arm. For a moment, he looked very old, very worn.

"Your Majesty, please, you shouldn't have come," the doctor insisted. "You should be resting."

The king ignored him. "And this is the way you found him?" he asked Russell.

Again, Russell wished he could have done something about Reginald's appearance for the king's sake. But all he could do was nod. "Yes, Your Majesty."

Every syllable was shrouded in grief's dark colors. "Naked and dead?"

If there had been some way to excuse it, Russell would have pounced on it. But there wasn't. He knew that finding Reginald this way somehow only heightened the tragedy, the waste. "Yes, Your Majesty."

Weston sighed and shook his head. "Too long," he repeated, more to himself than to anyone else in the room. "Too long. I've lived too long."

"Your Majesty, about that sedative now—" the doctor began.

"I don't want a sedative," Weston said with such feeling that it gave Russell hope the monarch was rallying. "I want my son. I want answers. Carrington, call the constable," he ordered.

"Yes, Your Majesty." Dutifully, Russell took out his phone again.

* * *

Jonas Abernathy was the royal constable, a jovial, affable man who, when he had initially been hired twenty-two years ago, had known police procedures like the back of his hand. However, in all the years he had been in the king's service, he'd had very little chance to put his knowledge to use. His wealth of knowledge had faded until it was little more than a memory.

He and his two assistants reminded Russell of small-town officers. Though the country had its own police force, it was more for show and for parades than anything else. Crime was not a problem in Silvershire. A little theft, a few arguments that had gotten out of hand and once a jealous husband who had shot both his wife and himself, missing both times. There'd never been a murder on record in Silvershire.

As he watched the three men conducting the investigation, Russell knew that they would not be equal to the task if the prince turned out to be a victim of homicide rather than his excesses. They were going to need someone good and someone discreet to handle this.

Russell waited until they were on their way out of the mansion, following the prince's covered body as it was being taken to the ambulance, before he said anything. He stood back with the king as the driver and physician lifted the gurney into the rear of the vehicle.

"Your Majesty, perhaps you might want to employ a more sophisticated agency to look into this matter for you." When the king made no reply, he continued, "I know of an organization that is very discreet."

As if rousing himself from an unnaturally deep sleep, Weston rendered a heartfelt sigh before finally answering. "Yes, you're probably right. Abernathy and his two will never get to the bottom of this if it is the slightest bit involved." Inside the ambulance, Dr. Neubert extended his hand to him, but rather than take it, the king suddenly turned to Russell. "Where were the bodyguards while this was happening? Where are they now?" he demanded heatedly. "Where were the people who were supposed to keep my son safe?"

"That will be one of the first things that will be addressed," Russell promised. The absence of the men who usually surrounded the prince had struck him as odd from the moment he'd discovered the body.

Finally taking the hand that the doctor offered, the king climbed into the rear of the ambulance, to take a seat beside his son. To grieve over the eyes that would never again open to look at him.

He turned to look at Russell before seating himself. "All right, I leave it in your hands, Carrington. Have it looked into. Find someone to do this for me, to bring me all the answers. I need to know what happened."

Russell already knew who he would approach. There was an organization known as the Lazlo Group. It was an international agency that could be trusted to be both professional and thorough in their investigation. They did not come cheaply, but they were well worth it. The organization guaranteed results and from what he had picked up abroad, the Lazlo Group always delivered on its promise.

"Right away, Your Majesty."

Russell stood back as the driver moved to close the ambulance doors. He caught one last look at the king. For a moment, Weston was not a ruler of a small, proud country, nor a man who had helmed that country into prosperity for the last thirty years. What Russell saw was a broken man.

"Is it true?"

Russell turned away from the fireplace. April dampness had brought a need for a fire to take the chill out of the air. Or perhaps, he mused, it was the circumstances that had rendered the chill and the fire was only an illusion to keep it at bay.

He'd followed the ambulance to the palace. A clinic was maintained on the premises, where the king or the prince could be seen when they weren't feeling well without being subjected to the public's prying eyes. The royal staff came there as well to be treated for things that were not of a serious nature. But now one of the clinic's three rooms had been converted into a makeshift morgue.

Russell had left the king there and gone to the receiving room to collect his thoughts. When he saw the fire, he'd been drawn to it. He'd wanted to warm himself somehow before calling the Lazlo Group.

He hadn't expected to run into anyone, least of all the princess.

Amelia crossed to the fireplace, waiting for an answer to the question that had been burning on her tongue for a number of hours. There had been rumors that the prince was dead, that he had been killed or had taken his own life. Any one of a number of unsettling theories were making their way through the palace, not to mention the news media, and she didn't know what to think.

The only thing she did know was there was one person in the palace she could trust to tell her the truth. Russell. The moment she'd heard he was back, she'd gone looking for him. One of the palace maids had sent her here.

Russell turned away from the fire. He tried to read her expression. Fear? Joy? Relief? He couldn't tell. She had the princess thing down to a science, he couldn't help thinking. Her expression was unreadable.

"Is what true?"

A guttural sound of disgust managed to escape her lips. "Don't play the game with me, Carrington. You're the one person I'm counting on to tell me the truth. Is it true?" she repeated. "Is the prince dead?"

"Yes."

Even though she'd been the one to ask the question, it took Amelia a second to process his answer. Reginald was dead. Dreading the very idea of marriage to him, she still found it hard to wrap her mind around the concept that he was gone, that he no longer posed a threat to her independence, to her happiness.

It took her breath away.

That he was dead meant that she was free. But at the same time, it meant that her homeland would continue to be at risk because it did not have the protection of a larger country.

Mixed emotions assaulted her, each tugging her in a different direction.

"How?" She took a breath before lengthening the question. "How did he die?"

Russell almost asked if she was sure she wanted to know the details. But she was not the delicate princess of old, too sensitive to know the truth. He wasn't going to insult her by keeping her in the dark.

"Not violently. At least," he amended, "there were no bruises, no marks on his body."

But a professional assassin would know where to land blows where they might not be detected at first, Amelia thought.

"That you could see," she corrected.

The hint of a smile that curved his lips had no humor in it. "I could see a great deal." Despite everything, he found himself pausing. Even though he thought of her as capable and intelligent, he kept finding himself wanting to protect her, to shield her from the nastier side of life. "Are you sure you want me to continue?"

Her eyes darkened. "I'm not a child, Carrington. Nor was there any affection lost between the prince and myself. I think you know that." Whatever he told her wasn't going to reduce her to tears. Disdain, maybe, but not tears. He had to be aware of that.

Russell forged ahead. "I found the prince in bed. He was naked."

Somehow, that didn't surprise her. It was in keeping with Reginald's reputation. More than ever, she felt like someone who had just dodged a bullet. But for the moment, the world would see the man as her fiancé. That meant that there would be humiliation by associ-ation. "I see. Was there anyone—?"

She didn't have to finish. Russell knew what she was asking. "No, the prince was alone when I found him. Very alone," he emphasized. When she raised a quizzical brow, he added, "There wasn't anyone in the entire mansion."

That almost seemed impossible. In photographs of Reginald, he had always been surrounded by people. He had a huge entourage following him wherever he went. That they were gone could only mean one thing. "Rats leaving a sinking ship?"

Most of Reginald's hangers-on were less than savory. The ones employed by the crown were supposed to be more steadfast, but fear could send troops scattering. It all depended on what had happened in the last few hours. Russell intended to get answers. "I suppose that's as good a guess as any."

Amelia studied his face, trying to discern his thoughts. Trying not to have any of her own that were unseemly at a time like this. But then, she had never loved Reginald, hadn't even liked him. If she felt no grief at his passing, only relief, she could be excused for that. "But you don't think his death was natural."

"No, I don't," he admitted. "The prince was thirty years old and as healthy as a horse."

The prince brought another kind of animal to mind as far as she was concerned. "He also behaved like a rutting pig."

"That kind of behavior could have gotten him a knife in his back," Russell pointed out. "It wouldn't have killed him like a silent thief in the night."

Amelia paused, thinking. The prince was given to excesses of all kinds. Alcohol, women, drugs. According to more than one article she'd read, life had to be one continuous party, or Reginald was bored. "It could have been an overdose."

"Possibly." It was the first thing he'd thought of, but he wasn't satisfied with that explanation. "But I've seen the prince consume enough alcohol for two men and still remain standing. He had an incredible tolerance for both alcohol and recreational drugs." He shook his head. "Something isn't adding up."

If it turned out that natural causes hadn't taken him and he hadn't accidentally died by his own hand, then the only conclusion to be drawn was that the prince had been murdered. The thought made her uneasy. When one royal was struck down, they were all vulnerable. Unless it was personal. "Who stands to gain from his death?"

"I was thinking more of the people who actively disliked him."

She laughed softly to herself. She wasn't the only one who had dodged a bullet today. Silvershire had been spared, as well. "From what I hear, that could be most of the country. Since he was Weston's only heir, who is next in line for the crown?"

Until she asked, he hadn't even thought about the immediate consequences of Reginald's death. Or what that meant to him, personally. Since the prince had been so vibrant, the idea that Reginald might not be around to ascend the throne had never even occurred to him.

But now that it did, he found the notion appalling. He had always disliked notoriety. It had only gotten more intense as he had grown older and placed more value on his privacy. Russell's expression was grim as he replied, "I am."

Her eyes widened as she felt her heart jump. She hadn't known that. She'd had no reason to know that. "You?"

He nodded. "According to the rules of succession of Silvershire. Weston ascended the throne because King Dunford had no sons, no children of his own. There were two dukes he felt were equal to the task. Everyone felt he was leaning toward Lord Benton Vladimir. But then he suddenly changed his mind and chose Weston to be the present king."

Thoughts she didn't want to entertain began whispering along the perimeter of Amelia's brain. And if she could think them, so could others who were less charitable. Others who didn't love Russell.

Amelia pressed her lips together as she looked at him. "If the prince died under suspicious circumstances—if he was murdered—someone might think that you had something to do with it."

She thought about the night they had spent together. Had that prompted Russell to rethink his position and take matters into his own hands? Was she the reason behind what had happened to the prince? Or could Russell have conceived an elaborate plan to capture the crown and she had blindly played into his hands?

No! How could she even think that way? Amelia upbraided herself. Russell was too honorable a man to be guilty of something like that. She was willing to bet her life on that.

On what? a small voice demanded. On a man she hardly knew? On a boy who used to put bugs into her bed? She didn't really know the man who stood before her, she reminded herself. She only knew the boy he had been. A great many years had come and gone between then and now.

Amelia felt torn. Logic pointed one way, but she refused to believe that her heart would have led her astray like that. There was goodness in Russell, she could see it in his eyes, feel it in his touch. She had no answer for it; she just did.

His eyes met hers. "Do you?" He couldn't tell what she was thinking. Something froze inside him. "Do you think I had something to do with it?"

"No."

Amelia had hesitated for a moment. If she'd believed in him, she wouldn't have, he thought. "But you're not sure."

She knew that protests were useless. He could see right through her. She could only tell him the truth. "Can I swear to it in a courtroom on a stack of Bibles? No. Because I don't have any way of actually knowing where you were every moment. But do I doubt your loyalty to the crown? No. Do I think that you are a murderer? No."

His eyes held hers for a long moment as he thought of the night they'd spent together. The night that should never have happened.

"My loyalty to the crown could come under question," he reminded her quietly.

She drew her shoulders back. "That wasn't a matter of loyalty."

That was exactly a matter of loyalty, he thought. "Then what was it?"

"A matter of two kindred spirits coming together." From out of nowhere, a thought occurred to her. "Or was that out of pity?" she asked suddenly.

"What?"

Amelia shook her head. She was just being over-wrought, she thought. She shouldn't have said anything. "Never mind."

But he didn't want to let it drop. "No, what did you mean by that? Was there anything that entire time that could make you suspect what happened was even remotely inspired by an emotion as condescending as pity?"

He sounded hurt, offended. She hadn't meant for any of that to happen. "No. I'm sorry. This whole situation is extremely distressing. I came here to be married to a man whose reputation I loathed—since he's gone, I don't see the point in hiding that," she said in response to the look in his eyes. "Now that he's dead, am I free of my obligation? Or am I, by default, betrothed to the next man in line?" She looked at him. "To you."

He measured out his words evenly. There seemed to be no emotion behind them. "Would that be so terrible?"

She took a breath. To his surprise she said, "That all depends."

"On what?"

"On how you feel about it."

He couldn't gauge by her voice how she felt about it herself. "How do you think I feel?"

Her temper came very close to breaking. "If I knew, would I be asking? A wondrous night of lovemaking does not automatically mean you want a lifetime of those nights. Sometimes magic is just that, magic. Meant for a hour, a night, not forever."

"So you're saying you wouldn't want to have to marry me."

Why did she suddenly feel like weeping? That wasn't like her, but she was so tired of being a pawn. "I'm saying I don't want to *have* to marry anyone, just as you don't want to be told who to marry. Marriage is a commitment that should come from the heart, not from a committee. The piece of paper involved should be a marriage certificate, not a treaty between two countries. I am a person, not a pawn." And then, like someone waking up from a bad dream, she stopped and blew out a breath. "I'm sorry, I had to get that out."

Russell inclined his head. "I understand, Princess."

She pressed her lips together again, impatience, frustration and a host of other emotions vying for control over her.

"'Princess,'" she echoed, shaking her head. "We are embroiled in intrigue, in murder and in heaven knows what else. We've slept together and might very well be married to each other before the week is out. My name is not 'Princess,' my name is Amelia."

The unexpected noise behind her sent adrenaline racing throughout her body. Amelia swung around to see that her father had entered the room and with him were several of his men. His complexion was flushed. Had he overheard her?

Chapter 10

Startled, it took Amelia a moment to rally. Since she acted as her country's representative in a great many diverse situations, her training under fire had been extensive. No one would have guessed that inside, she was still the young girl who had once tried so desperately to curry her father's favor.

Aware that the king had to have heard at least the end of her conversation with Russell and knowing that her father was far from a stupid man, she assumed he had put two and two together. But now was not the time to be upbraided for "conduct unbecoming." She was quick to throw the focus onto something that really mattered.

"Father, have you heard about the prince?"

The king's expression was grim as he nodded. "Terrible thing. Terrible thing," he repeated. "King Weston is beside himself. I tried to do what I could to comfort him, but this is a matter that will take a great deal of time for him to come to grips with. I'm told he collapsed when he received the news."

Russell felt a pang of guilt, but since the king had not addressed the remark to him, he said nothing.

"Reginald was his only son." Amelia moved so that she stood with her back to Russell, blocking him from her father's access. This was a private matter, but since it concerned Russell, she couldn't very well ask him to leave. And her father's bodyguards had been with the king for years. They were more like fixtures than men. Amelia drew herself up, asking a question she felt, in her heart, she already knew the answer to. "Will we be going home now, Father?"

Her father looked at her, a puzzled expression furrowing his brow. Behind her, she could almost feel Russell's gaze penetrating her back. "Why?"

"Because we came for a wedding and now that Reginald is dead—"

Roman cut her off. "Prince Reginald is dead," he agreed. "However, the alliance between Gastonia and Silvershire can and will still go forward." He looked at her intently, his gaze telling her she knew what was expected of her. "All that is needed for that to happen is for you to marry the next king of Silvershire."

Something inside her felt as if it was shattering. She was tired of being the good little obedient princess, tired of always doing what was expected of her. "And if that were a pig, would you have me take its cloven hoof in my hand and pledge to be faithful to the pig until the end of my days?"

Shock registered on her father's face. It echoed in the faces of his two bodyguards. She had no doubt that behind her, Russell didn't look like the picture of tranquillity, either. But she didn't care if any of them were shocked. There was a great need for her to speak her mind.

For a moment, the king looked as if he didn't know what to do with her. But when he spoke, his voice was patient. "You're overwrought, Amelia. I understand. However, nothing has really changed in the absolute sense. You have to think of the good of your people. Gastonia is a small, relatively defenseless country. Without the armed support of Silvershire, it could easily be taken over by any one of a number of countries. You are a princess, you cannot think with your heart." And then Roman looked at the tall man standing behind his daughter. "And, from what I just heard, as well as information that has been brought to me," he emphasized, "I believe a union between you two would not be entirely displeasing to either of you." He looked directly at Amelia and color crept up into her cheeks. Roman continued. "That the walls have ears is not merely an antiquated expression, my dear. I daresay that everything we do, whether we believe it's in private or not, becomes a matter of record." His meaning was quite clear as he looked from his daughter to the man he assumed would be king. "In addition to the main necessity for this marriage, for the sake of your reputation, Amelia, this marriage has to go through. Are we agreed, Carrington?"

Although his question was directed at Russell, it

was Amelia who ran interference. "It might seem a little callous to the people of Silvershire if the wedding goes ahead on schedule, only with a different groom."

Roman dismissed the idea. "Nonsense, the people love a fairy tale." His expression became serious. "What they wouldn't like is turmoil and unrest. Having the well-beloved princess marry the good Duke of Carrington will be just what they like, what they need. Gastonia will have its treaty and you will have a man you have already shown a preference for. And you, Carrington," he spared Russell a look, "will have your crown."

If the monarch only knew how little that meant to him, Russell thought. He knew the time for him to speak was now rather than later. "What if I don't want the crown?" Russell posed.

Roman looked at him as if he had just said that he had a strong desire to be flogged. "Not want the crown? How absurd. Dear boy, everyone wants the crown."

Russell had been taught to agree with royalty. To acquiesce whenever possible. But it wasn't possible. Not if there was a chance that he did not have to submit to this. He wanted a way out. Not because of a forced marriage, but because of a forced coronation.

"I don't," he said simply. "There's far too much attention attached to it. It would mean living the rest of my life in a fishbowl."

The king laughed shortly, shaking his head as if he was suffering someone who was simpleminded.

"You are already in that bowl, son. And as for not wanting the crown, I'm afraid you have no say in the matter. The rules are written," he pointed out. "And so is your destiny."

"The rules," Russell respectfully reminded him, "say that the king can change his mind."

Roman exchanged looks with his daughter. There would be no help coming from that quarter. He might as well squelch Carrington's hopes quickly, before they got out of hand.

"Right now, King Weston doesn't know his mind at all. He is in the terrible place that grief takes a man. He and I have been friends a very long time—since before you were born," he told his daughter. "In his time of grief, I know he would want me to keep things moving forward and move forward they shall." There was a note of finality in his voice as he spoke for the other monarch. "You will marry Carrington, Amelia, and Carrington will be the next king. I will hear no more about it."

So saying, King Roman swept out of the room with his bodyguards following closely behind him.

The room was very quiet for a moment. All that was heard was the sound of their breathing.

And then, because he couldn't bear the position he found himself in, couldn't bear the thoughts that were assaulting him, Russell broke the silence. "I could disappear," he offered.

Amelia stared at him, uncomprehending. This was his homeland. "Why would you do that?"

As if it wasn't written all over her face, he thought. As if her doubt wasn't palpable. "To spare you. You obviously don't want to go through with the ceremony."

Didn't he understand what he was suggesting? "If

you 'disappear,' people will think that you killed the prince and succumbed to the guilt."

"If I stay and marry you they might be inclined to think the same thing." It was damned if you do, damned if you don't, he thought. Except that until a few seconds ago, he had known which way he would have chosen to be damned. Now, he wasn't so sure and it hurt more than he was prepared for.

"Which would you rather do?" There wasn't so much as a hint in his eyes, she thought.

He shrugged his shoulders, looking away. "It doesn't seem that really matters to anyone."

How could he say that after the other night? She moved so that she was in front of him again. "It matters to me."

He wasn't sure if he truly believed that. Not after the uncertainty he'd seen in her eyes. He gave her his honest answer. "Then, Princess, I would rather marry you—and not be king."

He really meant that, she realized. That made him a unique man. "That doesn't seem to be a choice that's on the table."

"It should be." She couldn't read the expression that came over his face. "But then, if I wasn't to be king, you couldn't marry me, could you?"

Her heart froze as the thought she didn't want to entertain returned to haunt her. Could knowing that she had to marry the future king of Silvershire make Russell kill Reginald?

Oh, God, how could she think he was guilty of murder? The man she had made love with was gentle, tender. The hands that had touched her so reverently weren't the hands of a killer.

Were they?

"No," she answered quietly. "I couldn't. Not after my father had pledged my hand to the future king. But I could spare you," she went on to suggest. He looked at her quizzically. "If I were the one to run away, you couldn't marry someone you couldn't find."

Unable to resist the desire to touch her, he took her hand in his. "There's no need for you to run away. You're not the bad part of the bargain—the crown is." He brought her hand to his lips and kissed it. "And your father's right. If the public knows about us, or learns about us in the near future, then marriage to me is your only option."

Was that it? No mention of love, of desire, even of affection? Just some old-fashioned sense of duty? She pulled her hand away and tossed her head. "I don't have to safeguard my reputation, Carrington. This isn't a hundred years ago."

It wasn't all that easy to shake off the mantle of royal expectations. "Then why are you to marry the next ruler of Silvershire?" Russell asked gently.

Momentarily stumped, Amelia blew out a breath. "Point taken."

Touching her hand wasn't enough. He wanted to take her into his arms, to kiss her and make love with her. But now, of all times, they had to keep a distance between themselves. Besides, he reminded himself, she harbored suspicion in her soul. He had to remember that and not let himself be ruled by his hormones. Or his needs.

He began to back away from her, out of the room. "Princess, if you'll excuse me, I have a great many things to do."

She wanted to ask him to stay. To hold her. To tell her one last time that he had nothing to do with the prince's death. Her heart said one thing, her mind, taught to be suspicious, said another.

And she had also been taught to keep a tight rein on her emotions, so she merely inclined her head as he took his leave, saying nothing to stop him from going.

Russell had never felt more trapped in his life. He did not want to be king. Not once, in all the time that he had been growing up, had he entertained the idea of being king, even in passing or in jest. Reginald was only a year older than he was, in excellent physical health and vital and vibrant. It had never entered his mind that Reginald would not someday take the crown and be King of Silvershire.

Even though he'd felt that the prince was the wrong person for the responsibility, he had not once thought that he would make a better ruler than Reginald. He hadn't thought about being ruler at all, despite all of his schooling and qualifications, despite the fact that he cared about matters of state and Reginald wasn't interested in anything larger than the bust size of the woman he was currently with.

He, a king.

The very idea would have been laughable if it weren't so equally painful, Russell thought as he made his way down the palace corridor. What kind of a ruler would he make, anyway? He had betrayed the most sacred of trusts. Asked to bring back his future king's bride, he had slept with her instead.

Not exactly qualifications for ascending the throne.

How could he possibly be expected to lead a country if he couldn't even lead himself? If he couldn't control himself? Just now, back in that room with the princess, in the middle of it all, he had found himself thinking how beautiful she looked. How much he wanted to make love with her. Fine thoughts to be having when the prince's body was barely cold.

Damn it, this wasn't a time for angst and self-doubt. This was a time for action. The prince was dead and his first priority was finding about the circumstances that had led up to that event. His second would undoubtedly involve generating some sort of a cover-up of those circumstances, if for no other reason than to save the king public embarrassment and humiliation. The monarch had suffered enough of that already, thanks to Reginald's escapades. Enduring more of the same was not something that the king should be asked to go through.

There were intrigue and tangled webs no matter which way he turned, Russell thought. The fact that there wasn't a single living soul at the prince's estate was odd, to say the least. Reginald had always been surrounded by hangers-on and parasites. And there was the matter of the royal bodyguards. Where were they? Why hadn't they remained with the prince? He doubted very much that they had scattered of their own volition. Had Reginald ordered them away? Or had they been done away with in order to get to the prince? These and other questions begged for answers.

What had happened in the time he'd been away in Gastonia, making preparations to bring the princess back to Silvershire?

And losing his heart in the bargain, he added ruefully.

Russell sighed quietly to himself as he made his way up the spiral staircase. It was a damnable offense against all that he was raised to believe in, but in the shadowy recesses of his heart, he had to admit that he was relieved that Amelia was no longer going to have to marry Reginald for the sake of duty. The late prince would never have loved her, never have treated her with the kind of respect she deserved as a princess and as a human being.

His head throbbed. In a perfect world, he would have been able to marry Amelia with no strings attached, with no stain of doubt and suspicion attached to the union. But the world, he had learned long before he became the prince's shadow, was far from perfect. And this present situation he found himself in was apparently the best that he could hope for. To take the crown if he hoped to take the princess.

And what of the princess? Would she ever look at him without wondering if he'd had a hand in Reginald's demise? More than anything, he wanted to wipe away the suspicion shimmering in her eyes that was in danger of becoming a wall between them.

Somehow, he promised himself, he would find a way to turn everything else around and make Amelia believe that he had nothing to do with Reginald's death.

That he even had to entertain the thought hurt. She should have believed, without being told, without having it proven to her, that he was innocent.

The way to prove his innocence, he knew, was to find out exactly what had happened down to the last-minute details. He needed to learn who was with the prince in those final days and hours. And most importantly, he needed to learn if any of those people had been instrumental in having the prince killed.

His steps had brought him before the king's suite of rooms. Given a choice, he would gladly have left the monarch to his grief, but time was of the essence and they needed to get things moving. He wasn't sure if the ruler had processed what he had told him earlier about securing the operatives of the Lazlo Group. His grief and shock could have erased all memory of the suggestion.

Russell raised his hand and knocked on the finely carved oak door. In a moment, Bostwick, the head of the king's bodyguards, opened the door. The man was six feet three inches in both directions and bore a striking resemblance to a bulldog. He stood glaring at Russell, his body blocking access to the room.

Russell couldn't help thinking that it was a lucky thing he wasn't easily intimidated. Otherwise, Bostwick's scowl would have sent him running to his own room. "Bostwick, I'd like to have a word with King Weston, please."

The burly man remained unmoved. "The king is not seeing anyone," the man replied in a voice that seemed to have made the journey from the bottom of his toes.

But Russell was not about to be put off, not this time. "Bostwick—"

"Is that Carrington?" The king's voice: high, thin and reedy. He caught himself thinking that it sounded as if the monarch had aged ten years in the last hour.

"Yes, Your Majesty, it's me. Carrington." Russell raised his voice in order to be heard. "I need to speak with you."

"Let him in, Bostwick."

When Russell walked in, the first thing he noticed was the king's appearance. The strain in the man's face was incredible. He looked as if he had been to hell and back, sacrificing his soul in the process. It was difficult to believe this was the same man who had calmly gone over some plans with him just last night, before this whole business had started.

"Sit down." He gestured toward a love seat. "What is it?"

"I think we should have the prince's death looked into as soon as possible."

"You said that earlier, at the estate," the king reminded him. A sad smile played along his lips. "What? You think that I'm so grief-stricken that I've lost the use of my mind? I told you to proceed then, so by all means, proceed. Have this investigated. And when you find those who left my son in his hour of need, I want a complete accounting." He ran his hand along his forehead, as if willing back the tears that continued to gather, threatening to unman him. "Do you have anyone in particular in mind?"

He half expected the duke to mention himself. Instead, Carrington said, "I know the name of an international agency, Your Majesty. They are impartial and their track record for getting results is excellent. It's called the Lazlo Group. Corbett Lazlo has a team of highly skilled operatives who—"

Weston was vaguely familiar with the name. It was

a covert group no government publicly admitted to knowing. To his knowledge, they took care of dirty laundry.

He suddenly felt very weary. Ever since he had been told of Reginald's death, he'd felt himself tottering on the brink of abysmal despair. "Whatever you say, Carrington. I leave it to you."

Russell inclined his head. "Yes, Your Majesty." He paused for a moment, searching for a way to broach the subject delicately. There was none. He was forced to forge ahead. "Has the royal medical examiner been sent for yet, Your Majesty?"

Weston looked at him, a lost look in his eyes. The next moment, it disappeared. "What?"

"The medical examiner," Russell repeated politely. "Have you sent for her?"

The king wandered over to a window that overlooked the courtyard. In darkness, there was nothing to look at but shadows. Shadows as dark as the bottom of his soul. "No."

"I could do that for you—"

Weston turned from the window and looked at the man he had always thought of as a second son. Even as the thought crossed his mind, he felt a pang of guilt. He had no son. Not anymore. "Why?"

He and Bostwick exchanged glances. It was the first time he recalled ever seeing compassion in the latter's eyes. The man had been with the king for several decades and although it was not obvious, he grieved for his ruler. "An autopsy will have to be conducted in order to determine the exact cause of death—" Russell began as tactfully as he could.

Horror registered on Weston's regal face. "You mean cut him open?"

Russell felt as if each word were made of lead as he uttered it. "I'm afraid that's the only way, Your Majesty."

"Hasn't the prince suffered enough?" Weston demanded. His voice broke.

"I promise you, sire, the prince won't feel anything," Russell told him.

Weston sighed, coming away from the window. "But I will. I will feel every cut, every incision." The king paused, trying to compose himself. "When the queen died two days after giving birth to Reginald, I thought I could never hurt as much as I did then, losing her. I thought that I could never feel as lost as I did at the moment when her last breath left her body." He turned to look at the young man who was destined to take his son's place. "I was wrong. I'm not sure how I am going to get through this, Russell. Not sure at all."

Russell drew closer to him, silently offering him his strength, grieving not for the prince, but for the father he had left behind. "You will get through it because you are the king. And a very strong man."

A bittersweet smile played along his lips. "Not so strong, Russell. Not so strong." He looked down at the framed photograph he was holding. It was of the prince, taken on his tenth birthday. Tears gathered in the king's eyes. "I should have stopped him. When he was getting out of control, I should have stopped him. Not indulged him. But I thought, hoped, that he would outgrow this reckless behavior.

"I had a bit of a wild streak myself before I was

made the king," he confided. "The weight of the crown sobers you. Makes you humble and makes you realize that your own wishes need to take a back seat to those of your people." His voice all but drifted away as he said, "I thought that would come to him, as well."

Obligation forced Russell to say words he didn't truly believe for the king's sake. "It might have."

"But now we'll never know."

"No, sire, we won't," Russell agreed. "But we can know what happened to him. I know he would want you to find out the truth and if there is someone responsible for all this, the prince would have wanted you to bring them to justice." He paused before adding, "Even if it means cutting him open."

Weston nodded. "You're right. Call this Lazlo. Tell him I want to find out every detail, no matter how small and insignificant, of my son's last few days. Everything," he underscored.

"And the royal M.E.?" Russell prodded gently.

Weston squared his shoulders. He began to look a little like his old self. "I would like to hold off on that for a few days. Just until after the wedding day has passed. I can't explain it, I just don't want my son to be cut up into pieces on the day he should have been married, even if they do put him back together again." He looked at Russell for agreement, even though he did not expect to be contradicted.

Russell saw no reason to upset him further by pushing for a speedy autopsy. A few days shouldn't really matter, not if the events leading up to Reginald's death could be reconstructed. Reginald's autopsy could be postponed for a while and conducted at a later time.

Straightening his shoulders, Russell bowed before the king. "As you wish, Your Majesty."

"As I wish." Weston repeated the words. They rang ironically and mocked him as they drifted into oblivion. If things had gone according to his wishes, they would have arranged themselves so differently….

Pushing aside thoughts of weddings and coronations until he could better handle them, Russell quietly withdrew to place his call to Corbett Lazlo as Bostwick shut the doors.

Chapter 11

"And you suspect someone in the palace?"

The voice over the telephone was calm, resonant. It echoed slightly, the way voices over a speaker phone did. The echo did not diminish the effect. It was the same voice that had soothed distraught heads of state confronted with the kidnappings of loved ones. The same voice that had promised—and delivered—results in highly delicate government situations that the public had never even suspected.

Corbett Lazlo was a brilliant, enigmatic man very few people actually recognized. Those who did know him saw a tall, trim man with ice-blue eyes that conflicted with an almost boyish grin that even fewer were ever privy to. Some said he was an ex-CIA operative. Others claimed he was a bored genius with a love for challenges. Still others said he was the illegitimate son of a former French president and had cut his teeth on both foreign policy and espionage. No one knew for sure.

The only proven fact was that approximately twelve years ago, he had formed the Lazlo Group, an international team of highly skilled agents who specialized in, among other things, investigating the deaths of political figures.

The Lazlo Group was one of the best kept secrets of the free world. They were usually called in as a last resort, or when affairs were of such a delicate, discreet nature that no one else could be trusted to handle them.

Corbett Lazlo had no affiliation with any particular nation. He was a citizen of the world. His people did whatever was necessary to get the job done. There were never any questions asked by the party or parties who hired them. It was better that way.

The call Russell had placed to him had been rerouted several times so that Russell had no idea exactly where Corbett Lazlo was located. It was the way Corbett preferred it. Russell didn't care. Lazlo's location didn't matter. All that mattered was finding out the series of events that led up to Reginald's last day and death.

"I suspect everyone right now," Russell said, answering Lazlo's question. "Except for King Weston. And the princess," he added.

He heard what he took to be just the slightest chuckle on the other end.

"Never be too hasty in your judgment," Lazlo advised. "The princess stood to gain something from the prince's death."

Russell frowned. There had been a treaty riding on

the union. As far as he knew, there was nothing on the balance sheet if the prince died before they were married. "What?"

There was a pregnant pause on the other end, as if the man expected more of him. "Her freedom. Theirs wasn't exactly going to be a fairy-tale marriage. The prince went on whoring to the very end." He delivered the information as if he had been a witness to Reginald's behavior. Russell knew that the man kept himself informed on many fronts. "Not quite the behavior for a man who was about to be married to the woman of his dreams."

Russell could feel himself growing protective again. It had never occurred to him that Amelia might not need a champion, that she would want to fight her own battles at all times. He wouldn't hear her maligned, even theoretically. "She had nothing to do with it."

There was just a hint of indulgence in Lazlo's voice as he abandoned his point. "Nonetheless, we leave no stone unturned. My people don't come cheaply, Carrington, but they pride themselves on delivering. Everything," he emphasized. "The good and the bad."

"Money isn't a problem." He knew he spoke for the king when he made the affirmation. The monarch would have no peace until the matter of his son's death was resolved. And perhaps, sadly, not even then.

"Good. I'll be sending one of my top operatives to the palace. Her name is Lucia Cordez." Lazlo's voice was quick, staccato, leaving no room for argument as he took command of the situation. "You will invite her to the wedding. She will blend in."

About to protest that there would be no wedding,

Russell was suddenly struck by a thought. "How will I know her?"

"Trust me, you'll know her. She has the disadvantage of being stunning." A disadvantage, because he preferred his operatives to blend in rather than stand out. But he couldn't hold Lucia's beauty against her, not when she was so skilled at what she did. "Don't let her looks fool you. She's good under pressure and she is a computer expert."

That out of the way, Russell questioned the scenario that Lazlo was painting. "The wedding is canceled."

"Check your scorecard. There's been a substitution play. The wedding hasn't been canceled, just recast. Playing the part of the prince will be Russell, Duke of Carrington. Don't you pay attention to your traditions, Carrington?" When he received no response, there was a note of satisfaction in the older man's voice as he continued. "You're paying me to be informed. You're also paying me to find the truth." Again Lazlo paused, this time so that his words could sink in one at a time. "One could say that you had a great deal to gain from the prince's death."

Russell laughed to himself. Lazlo had no idea how absurd that idea was, he thought. "Feel free to investigate me."

"Thank you." His tone indicated that they would have done just that with or without permission. "We'll be in touch, Carrington."

With that, the conversation was terminated.

Russell replaced the receiver and stood for a moment, staring at the telephone, not seeing it. Not seeing anything at all in the study.

He was getting married. In less than a day if everything was held to the same schedule as before.

He had no idea how he felt about that. Other than numb.

Amelia adjusted her headpiece. The veil wasn't falling the right way. She felt tears gathering in her eyes and knew that they had nothing to do with the veil.

Tension brought the tears.

Things were happening much too fast for her. She'd never been one to enjoy life in the slow lane, but this was far more than she had bargained for. Far more than she could assimilate.

Her head felt as if it were spinning.

Less than two weeks ago, she had been in her gardens, fervently wishing that time would somehow find a way to stand still, at least for a little while. Dreading the wedding that loomed before her on the horizon like some creature that had been resurrected in a mad scientist's laboratory.

And now, despite all the changes, despite the royal tragedy of finding the prince dead in his bed, the wedding was still going to be on schedule. Only the groom had been changed.

She was marrying Russell.

Just the way, in a moment filled with passion and desire, she'd wanted to. Just the way she'd wished. Russell, who had introduced her to the world of love-making. Russell, who had grown into a man who was, at the core, kind and gentle and caring.

Russell, who now looked at her with distant eyes.

She knew it was because, in an unguarded moment, she'd allowed herself to tell him the truth. Tell him that, for less than a fragment of a second, she'd had doubts about him.

Dear lord, she had doubts about herself, as well. Doubts about everything right now.

But men didn't understand the emotional distress that women sometimes found themselves laboring under. Men didn't understand how women thought with their hearts as well as their heads.

Logic was the only thing that made sense to a man like Russell. And when confronted with what he thought to be the logic of her suspicions, he'd shut down. Shut her out. Grown distant.

In the last day and a half, when she'd tried to reach him, tried to get him alone just to talk to him, he had brushed her off by saying that he was too busy. He seemed to go out of his way to make himself unavailable to her.

If she didn't know any better, she would have said that he was trying to avoid her.

She adjusted the headpiece for the dozenth time. She stared at her reflection, not seeing the elaborate beadwork that had taken seamstresses weeks to complete. Maybe, she thought, she did know better.

Maybe he *was* trying to avoid her because she'd committed the sin of suspecting him. Or was it because she was right, and avoiding her until the ceremony was the only way he could handle the problem?

Was Russell involved in the prince's death?

The question kept haunting her, and every time she

thought she'd put it to rest, it insisted on rising up again, like fabled ghosts on All Hallows' Eve.

She sighed and stared blindly into the mirror, fervently wishing she could see into the future. Her future. Even if only into the next few weeks.

Amelia pressed her hand against her stomach. She hadn't eaten anything all morning. It seemed to her, as each half hour passed, that the butterflies that had taken up residence there grew a little larger.

"You are gorgeous." Amelia raised her eyes and focused. Madeline had entered the room, leaving the other bridesmaids in another room, and come up behind her. The woman paused to straighten out her train. "All except for the sad face, of course," she observed matter-of-factly. "Looking at your expression, you'd think that you were still marrying Reginald, The Black Prince, instead of Bonnie Prince Russell."

Amelia lifted her head, still keeping her face toward the mirror. Praying that Madeline couldn't see the hint of tears. "He's not a prince yet."

"Po-tay-to, po-tah-to," Madeline quipped. "Carrington is going to be king once the coronation takes place. Technically, that makes him a prince." Madeline indulged her. "Or a prince-in-waiting, if you prefer. Besides, if I remember correctly, you thought of him as your Prince Charming not all that many days ago." She shifted so that she could see Amelia's face for herself, rather than just the reflection. "Trouble in paradise already?"

Amelia shook her head. The headpiece wobbled. Madeline made a disapproving, clucking sound as she straightened it again.

"It's just too fast, that's all."

"Too fast," Madeline echoed. "Did I miss something?" she wanted to know. "Switching your emotions from loathing and dread to whoopee shouldn't be all that difficult."

It was fine for Madeline to make jokes about it. Madeline wasn't being served up on a tray named Diplomacy. "I can't shake the feeling that I'm still being used as a pawn."

Like Amelia, Madeline had grown up around politics all of her life and had made it a point to pay close heed. Unseduced by the glamour of a fairy-tale wedding, she knew exactly what was happening.

Slowly, she surveyed Amelia from all angles. The ceremony was set to begin in a few minutes. "By your father? Obviously. But since the king on the chessboard is Carrington instead of Reginald, being captured shouldn't be something to drag your feet about."

"No, I mean by Carrington. I feel, no, I mean I'm afraid," Amelia amended, "that he might be using me as a pawn."

"Carrington?" Surprise and amusement played along her face. "Amelia, think. Carrington doesn't need you to become king. He doesn't need an alliance with Gastonia to put him on the throne. But *you* need *him* to protect Gastonia from dreadful little countries like Naessa, remember?"

But the fear refused to go away. Because Russell had kept his distance, it had gotten a toehold on her and insisted on festering.

She drew Madeline close to her and lowered her

voice. "What if, after our night together, Russell decided to have the prince killed?"

Madeline's eyes met hers. Amelia couldn't tell what she was thinking. And then she saw that quirky smile she was so familiar with that lifted only one corner of her friend's mouth. The one that mocked her good-naturedly. "My, my, and don't we have the swelled head? Just how good do you think you were in bed?"

Amelia sighed, waving a hand. Madeline was right. She was overthinking this. It was just that it all seemed so surreal to her. "I guess I'm just confused."

Still looking at her in the mirror, Madeline placed her hands on her friend's shoulders and gave her a little comforting squeeze. "Honey, Carrington is crazy about you. Anyone looking at him can see that. This is a good thing, I promise." Releasing, her, Madeline stepped back. "Just this once, it looks as if your fairy godmother has really come through for you. Enjoy it. Enjoy him." Madeline's quirky smile made a return appearance. "Or if you don't want to, I will gladly become your second string and you can send me in to take your place."

The tension broke and Amelia began to laugh, really laugh. She laughed so hard that she found herself holding on to her sides. "Oh God, that felt good. What would I ever do without you, Madeline?"

Born without a single bone of conceit in her body, Madeline assured her, "You'd muddle through. It would just take you a little longer, that's all." Familiar chords began to resonate over the intercom in the vestibule. It was time. Madeline gave Amelia an encouraging smile. "I think they're playing your song, Princess."

The butterflies in her stomach made a quantum leap, butting wings against one another. Amelia's hand flew to her stomach and she pressed against it, feeling as if she was going to throw up. "Oh, God."

"Just smile and look gorgeous," Madeline advised. "And remember to say 'I do' in the right place." Bending, she shifted Amelia's train so that she could walk out of the small room. "Just remember, this could have been Reginald and thank your lucky stars that you wound up dodging that bullet."

Amelia opened the door. The other bridesmaids, a mixture of women she'd known since childhood and daughters from prominent families, all began talking at once.

The sound formed a wall of noise around her. Amelia forced a smile to her lips and froze it there as she exited the small room.

It was time to meet her destiny.

He looked so stern, Amelia thought as she approached Russell and the altar in rhythmic, measured steps, her hand resting lightly on her father's arm. Shouldn't he be smiling?

Russell stood by the minister who was officiating at the ceremony. Close beside him was the king, taking his place as the best man. She knew that the monarch had insisted on it because it made him feel closer to Reginald. Right next to Weston were the groomsmen.

All she could really see was Russell.

His face looked rigid, as if he were waiting for a battle cry instead of his bride-to-be.

Fear ran in on spiked cleats. Was this a mistake? Should she have insisted on having the ceremony canceled, or at the very least, postponed, until matters between them had been ironed out?

Until the matter of whether or not the prince had been murdered was resolved?

Any way she looked at it, this just didn't seem like the ideal time to get married. The whole country, not to mention the relationship between the two of them, was in a state of chaos. Yet here she was, approaching the altar, about to say the words that would officially join their two countries, their two destinies.

Something inside Amelia wanted her to raise her skirts, turn on her heel and run as fast as she could to the nearest exit. But she didn't do any of that, she continued approaching the altar. Approaching Russell.

Despite everything, she thought, as King Roman placed her hand in Russell's, she loved him. That much she was certain of. No matter what he might be guilty of, she loved Russell.

For better or worse.

The words had added significance to her as she heard them being said by the minister. She repeated them, cadence for cadence, glancing up only briefly at the man she said them to.

Russell's expression remained unreadable. She could feel the frost forming around her heart.

Lucia Cordez, dressed in a stunning, blue streetlength dress that lovingly adhered to every supple curve her finely trimmed, martial-arts-trained body had to offer, dabbed subtly at her light blue eyes as she pretended to be moved by the ceremony she and so many others were attending.

No one had questioned her presence. With a Latin father and a mother who was half African American, half Caucasian, and blessed with model-perfect good looks, Lucia had the kind of face and bearing that easily allowed her to fit in anywhere people of quality gathered.

She'd arrived in Silvershire a little more than an hour ago, just in time to catch Carrington before he left for the church. She'd put a few pertinent questions to the duke, the most important of which was whether he knew the whereabouts of the late prince's laptop. He'd had the presence of mind to place it under lock and key within his own room.

Lucia had commended him for his action and taken possession of the key. The moment the reception got underway, she intended to make herself scarce and get started hacking into the prince's computer files. Because Reginald had been Silvershire's future king, his files had been highly secured with intricate pass codes that only he had known. She had come prepared. Cracking them could take her a matter of hours, or it could take as long as several months. Optimistically, she hoped for somewhere in between.

There was no time like the present to get started. But, for the moment, Lucia allowed herself to enjoy the wedding. It was the last word in opulence. Silvershire was not without its resources. And she had always had a fondness for pomp and ceremony. It was leagues away from her own background.

It was what she aspired to.

It felt as if the reception would never end.

Part of Amelia had nursed the hope that it wouldn't, because part of her was afraid of this moment, when the reception was on its way to becoming just a memory and she was alone in the royal bedroom with her new husband. Not afraid the way she would have been just a few short days ago, but afraid because of the issue that had sprung up between her and Russell. The issue that still remained unresolved, at least for Russell. And maybe, just in the tiniest bit, for her.

She released the breath she was holding. This was absurd. They were married now. They were a united couple before God and the world. It was time to begin acting like one.

Amelia turned around to say something to Russell, who had remained almost eerily quiet since they'd left the ballroom and entered the bedroom. She was still acutely aware that he had refrained from carrying her over the threshold.

To her surprise, she saw that her brand-new husband was crossing back to the doorway. His hand was on the doorknob and he looked as if he intended to leave. A strange chill passed over her.

"Where are you going?"

He glanced in her direction. Wished she didn't look as beautiful as she did. Wished she didn't move him the way she did. She was still in her wedding dress, looking as pure as she should have been had he not given in to his earthier instincts. "To my quarters."

She stared at him, puzzled. "Aren't these your quarters?"

He didn't think of them in that way. He'd always felt himself a visitor in the palace, no matter how many nights he'd spent here. "They're the quarters reserved for the wedding night."

Because he hadn't moved away from the door, Amelia crossed to him, taking off her headpiece and veil as she approached. She tossed them onto a wing chair as she passed it.

"Correct me if I'm wrong." Amelia began to take the pins out of her hair. "But doesn't the wedding night follow the wedding?"

He watched, unable to draw his eyes away, as her hair came cascading down like sunbeams. "Yes."

Amelia ran her fingers through her hair, loosening the last of the trapped strands. "And weren't we the bride and groom involved in the wedding?"

His mouth felt dry. She was distracting him. He had to remember why he had been so determined to walk away. It wasn't easy. "Yes."

"Then these should be our quarters," she concluded, stopping less than a hairbreadth away from him. "Jointly."

He squared his shoulders. She was making this hard. "Princess—"

"Amelia," she corrected, trying to bank down the sudden spike of frustration that shot through her. "My name is Amelia." Despite her efforts, exasperation entered her voice. "Why won't you call me that? Do I have to give you a flash card?"

She had a point. It was something he was going to have to get used to. They were supposedly equals, now. "Amelia," he repeated. "There's no need for you to act out the charade."

She didn't follow him. "What charade? That we're married?"

He struggled to maintain the distance between them. "We don't have to behave like husband and wife."

"Why? Why don't we have to behave like husband and wife? Why wouldn't we want to behave like husband and wife?" she repeated, her temper heating.

Did he have to spell it out for her? "Because the first element in a marriage is trust and you obviously don't trust me—"

She had had just about enough of this. "No," Amelia cut in tersely. "You are the one who doesn't trust me."

For a moment, she'd taken the air out of his sails. "What? I—"

She wouldn't let him continue, wouldn't let him weave rhetoric until up was down and black was white. And as she spoke, her voice rose and anger came into her eyes, making them almost shoot sparks.

"You don't trust that I have common sense. You don't trust that my heart will convince my somewhat confused mind that you are a decent, good man who could never, ever, have anything to do with the prince's death. All you can do is shoot daggers at me and growl like some wounded, unforgiving bear." As she spoke, she poked a finger into his chest, emphasizing her words.

"I had a moment, a tiny moment, of doubt, of confusion. A lapse." She held her forefinger and thumb up, to show him how tiny the occasion had actually been for her. "What does a moment count in the scheme of things? One moment in the face of a billion moments that comprise a lifetime. *Our* lifetime, if you could get off your high horse and stop looking at me like some wronged soldier who—"

She never got to finish. Her words were inflaming him. *She* was inflaming him. Unable to resist her any longer, Russell pulled her into his arms.

The next second, her mouth was covered with his.

Chapter 12

What had just happened here?

Her pulse racing faster than could be measured by any earthly instrument, Amelia drew her head back to look at Russell.

"Have I gotten to you or are you just trying to shut me up?"

"Yes, and yes," he answered, a kiss to either side of her neck separating the two affirmations.

He'd been without her too long. It felt like a lifetime, even though logically he knew that by the calendar, it had only been a matter of a few days.

His blood heated to an almost unbearable point, Russell found that he didn't want to waste any more time, not with words, not with delays. Though nothing had really been resolved to his satisfaction, though he still felt hurt by Amelia's initial flash of distrust, he couldn't resist these demands storming through him any longer.

Still kissing her, he moved his hands to the back of her dress. He had only one goal in mind: to separate the heavily beaded gown from her body as quickly as humanly possible.

His goal was thwarted almost immediately. Instead of a zipper, his fingers came in contact with what felt like a army of tiny round buttons, marching up and down the length of her back in single file. They extended from her shoulder blades to well past her waist. There had to be over a hundred of them, he thought in utter frustration as he moved his head back to look at her.

Despite the fact that her skin felt as if it were sizzling, Amelia had to bite down on her lower lip to keep from laughing. The mystified look on her new husband's face was almost too adorable to withstand.

"You're bundled up like a national treasure," he complained. And then the frown left his lips. A look entered his eyes that would have completely captured her heart—if it hadn't already been his. "In a way, I suppose that you are."

It took effort not to simply melt into his arms at that point. "The royal dresser helped get me into this," she told him. There was no way she could have fastened all the buttons on her own.

"Well, I'm not calling her to help get you out. If I can't manage this on my own, I don't deserve to be the next King of Silvershire." With desire vibrating through him, growing in urgency by the moment, he had to focus in order to hold himself in check and not to rip the gown right off her body. "Turn around," he instructed.

"Yes, Your Majesty," she curtsied, a gleam in her eyes, before she turned and offered her back to him.

"Not yet," he reminded her. "I'm not king yet." His breath teased her spine as he removed one tiny button after another from its loop. It was slow going. Far slower than he was happy about. "This is worse than a chastity belt," Russell muttered under his breath.

She felt his hands along her skin, felt her body tightening and humming in anticipation. She found it difficult to breathe. Difficult to remain where she was instead of throwing herself into his arms and kissing him with abandon.

Standing as still as she could, her hands on her waist, Amelia glanced at him over her shoulder. "And just how many chastity belts have you removed?"

Why did there have to be so many buttons? A half-dozen would have been sufficient. His fingers were growing thick and clumsy as he kept repeating the procedure over and over again. "What?"

"You just said that the buttons were worse than a chastity belt. I was just wondering how many princesses you've liberated in your time."

"You would be the first," he told her.

And, he added silently, in a way, Amelia was liberating him. Freeing his soul with her sweetness from the solitary cell where it had been confined.

Nothing had changed. He still didn't want to be crowned king, still didn't want the attention that went with this very public role he was being forced to take on, but he did want this woman. Wanted her with the last fiber of his being. Wanted her more than he had first initially realized. And if that meant enduring public scrutiny beneath a blistering spotlight, so be it. He would find some way to deal with it.

So long as he could have her. All he cared about was having her, now. He was consumed with desire, with need.

It felt as if the space of time between when they had first made love and now was several decades instead of merely several days. His body longed for her. More, his soul longed for her, for the feel of the safe haven that existed in her arms, in her kiss.

"Done," he declared with no small note of triumph as he finally pushed the last tiny button out of its confining loop.

Rather than turn her around to face him, Russell slid the dress slowly from her shoulders, down her arms. All the while he had her against him and was kissing the slope of her neck, the soft expanse of her back. He heard her moan and it only served to fuel the fire that had already begun to rage inside him.

The fire that only she could quench.

This was amazing, Amelia thought. Russell was giving her goose bumps even as he was heating her body with his oh-so-clever mouth. She felt as if she were being consumed by both fire and ice at the very same time.

How was that possible?

When he cupped her breasts, still weaving a network of kisses that ran along her back, Amelia turned within the circle of his arms so that she could face him. Face him so that she could begin removing the formal uniform that he had worn to their wedding.

He'd looked so tall and brave, standing there at the altar in his uniform. Her soldier. Now all she wanted was to have him standing there without it.

Eager, wanting, Amelia tore aside the dress sash, pushed the jacket from his shoulders and all but ripped the shirt from his body.

All the while, her body cheered her on, silently crying, "More."

"Princess," Russell teased, a wide grin on his darkly tanned face, "are you attacking me?"

"With every fiber of my being," she breathed. "And it's Amelia. Amelia," she emphasized breathlessly for what felt like the umpteenth time. When would he stop thinking of her as a title and start thinking of her as a woman? His woman.

"Amelia," he repeated, his voice low, husky with unspent passion.

She could almost feel her name dance along her skin, encased in his breath. It drove her crazy.

Everything that came after was a blur, like the events in someone else's dream.

The rest of the clothing, both hers and his, wound up in a tangled heap of brocades, silks and beads on the floor—as tangled as their bodies swiftly became.

She couldn't get enough of him.

The more excitement rose within her body in an ever-heightening crescendo, the more Amelia found herself wanting more. Wanting him. She desperately wanted the sensation he had created within her to continue forever, or as close to forever as was humanly possible.

Russell did his best to accommodate her. His pleasure in part derived from the way Amelia moved beneath him, from the moans that escaped her lips as he familiarized his hands and then his lips with every inch of her body. With swift, clever, promising movements, he brought her to climax upon climax. To joy upon joy. Joy that, only a short while ago, had been completely unimagined for both of them.

Within the shelter of an evening, she became his kindred soul. He could read or sense everything she was experiencing. He could literally see it in Amelia's face. With little effort, he wrapped himself in it, experiencing the moment vicariously with her.

He'd forgotten how almost tooth-jarring falling in love—*making* love—could be.

Finally, unable to hold back any longer, feeling as if he would burst, Russell laced his hands with hers and raised them over her head. His eyes on hers, he lowered his body slowly until the imprint of hers was indelibly pressed against it.

And then he entered her.

This time, there was no small, almost imperceptible protest at the merging. No muffled whimper of pain that she tried to keep from him. This time, there was nothing but joy—for both of them.

The island of time that they had been allowed to carve out for one another faded away all too quickly. By ten the next morning, it seemed to have occurred almost a lifetime away, even though they had made love several times during the course of the night.

With daylight came obligations and matters to see to. They both knew that.

But still, she found herself wanting to break rules, to grab up her happiness with both hands and hold it to her before something or someone made it disappear.

She watched him as he got out of bed. Though she knew it was ridiculous, a hint of loneliness whispered along the edges of her consciousness. "No one would fault us if we remained here." She raised her eyes to his. "In our own private kingdom where the rest of the world has no access."

Russell leaned over her and pressed a kiss to her forehead. "You're wrong. It does have access." Before she could protest or ask what he meant, he lightly tapped her forehead where he had just kissed it. "Right there. It barges in at the least opportune time, demanding attention."

She supposed he was right. Reluctantly, Amelia rose, tossing aside the sheet that had covered her. She felt remarkably unselfconscious about the fact that she was nude. The nightgown that her dressmaker had designed especially for last night had never seen the light of day. It was still tucked away in the bureau drawer.

No one was more surprised than she at the way she felt. But right now, there was no shame, no embarrassment after the dew of afterglow had faded. She felt at ease like this with him.

It was as things should be, Amelia thought, crossing to the closet where members of the staff had already placed any garment that she could possibly want within easy access. Opening the door, she drew a dressing gown from its hanger. Slipping it on, she purposely left the two sides hanging open as she turned around to face him.

"If I had married Reginald, we would be on our way to our honeymoon. To Hawaii, where he would undoubtedly have hit on someone even as the bellboy was checking in our luggage." She raised her head slightly, her eyes on his as she smiled. "This is much better."

He had every intention of leaving the room. Of meeting with Lucia Cordez as had been arranged when she'd arrived yesterday. But the sight of Amelia's soft, inviting curves peering out from beneath the royal-blue silk robe completely destroyed his resolve as well as his game plan.

A man was only so strong and then no more.

What would a few more minutes hurt? It wasn't as if Corbett Lazlo's computer expert was going anywhere in the immediate future. For all he knew, Lucia hadn't been able to find anything yet. The password that Reginald had implemented on his files was, perforce, a bear to break. The late prince had been gleefully proud of that.

Reginald had implemented it not to keep the enemies of Silvershire from knowing any of his private affairs, or even his own personal enemies, but to make sure that his father remained in the dark about his less-than-noble activities.

At thirty years old, Reginald had been a child to the last breath in his body.

Russell couldn't help wondering now if, for some reason, some secret piece of information on his computer could have ultimately been what had gotten Reginald killed. They might never find out.

The possibilities as to what had led to Reginald's death were endless. They could also be nonexistent. Either way, if Lucia had come up with an answer, it would keep for a few more minutes. Perhaps even for half an hour.

If he could get his fill of Amelia in that amount of time.

It amazed him, after the night they had spent together, that he still had any energy left to walk, much less to make love with her again. He knew his limitations and he had never been a machine, the way Reginald boasted that he was. But Amelia seemed to bring out a supply of hidden reserves he hadn't even been aware of possessing, he thought with a grateful smile.

"Yes," he agreed, crossing to the closet where she stood and slipping the robe from her shoulders. The garment slid from her arms to the floor. "Much better."

Amelia rose up on her bare toes, brushing her nude body against his.

Again, everything tightened in anticipation even as drumrolls sounded up and down her limbs and her loins moistened. With a soft laugh, her eyes gleaming, she threaded her arms around his neck. Her body pressed closely against his ever-hardening one.

The next half hour was lost. As was the hour that came after.

"I'm sorry I'm late," Russell apologized as he strode into the conference room where Lucia had set up her temporary office.

He had just now finished buttoning his jacket. Russell didn't have to glance at his watch to know that it was close to noon, almost two hours later than he'd originally said he would come to speak with her. His hair was still damp in places from the shower he'd taken, the one that normally would have taken him less than five minutes. It, too, had fallen behind schedule because, at the last minute, Amelia had slipped into the stall with him.

He'd never enjoyed getting clean as much as he had this time.

Lucia Cordez raised the oversized glasses she used for reading and slid them onto the top her head, giving the duke her undivided attention. She was wearing a pair of cutoff denim shorts that showed her long legs off to their best advantage and a sleeveless light pink blouse that seemed more suited to the beach than to the dark business at hand.

He noticed that there was a plate with just the barest remnants of wedding cake on it and wondered if that had been her breakfast.

Lucia smiled at him. "Actually, you're earlier than I anticipated."

He didn't see how that was possible "I said ten o'clock."

The smile on Lucia's lips told him she knew better, even if he didn't. "You were married yesterday," she reminded him. "I didn't think you meant ten o'clock in actual real time. The cake was good, by the way. I wish I could steal your chef," she added wistfully.

He looked over her shoulder at the computer monitor on the table. The binary code that covered the screen looked like some kind of decorative screen saver. "You give me something I can work with, I'll have another wedding cake made for you."

She inclined her head as if to say that sounded fair enough. "Well, as it happens, I'm still working on the prince's monarch code."

He'd thought as much. Russell groaned, running his hand through his hair. Damn it, why had Reginald enjoyed that part of it so much? Was it because it made him feel as if he were acting his age instead of behaving like the eternal juvenile he always seemed to be?

"However," Lucia went on, "there is some good news, so to speak."

"And that would be—?" he asked, gesturing for her to continue.

"In looking for the encryption code, I stumbled across a sealed file on his computer." A small, triumphant smile crossed her lips. "It only took about half an hour to crack the password. When I opened the file, I saw that it contained a batch of personal e-mails." Lucia leaned back in her chair to look at him. She needed to see his face in order to gauge whether or not he was hiding something. It wasn't unheard of to have the client not altogether forthcoming when it came to an investigation. "Are you aware that Prince Reginald was being blackmailed?"

"Blackmailed?" Russell echoed, confused. That didn't make any sense. "What could they possibly have to blackmail him with? The photographers followed him everywhere. Everything about his sordid life was a matter of record."

"Apparently not everything, because the prince was making regular withdrawals from his private account. That usually means that regular payments were going somewhere. In addition, there's mention of several meetings, all coinciding with withdrawals. The sender also threatens to 'expose' the prince several times in case he was thinking of going to the authorities."

Russell began to wonder if there was anyone on Reginald's side. The list of people who had something against the man kept growing. He almost felt sorry for the late prince. "Do you have any idea who was blackmailing him?"

Lucia shook her head. "That I haven't found out yet. I haven't been able to trace the source of the e-mails—yet," she emphasized the word. "But I've only been at this for less than a day," she reminded him with the confidence of one who had had eventually met every single technological challenge she'd encountered.

By the expression on her face, Russell surmised that Lazlo's operative was not in the habit of making excuses or feeling that she needed to.

"Anything else?" he asked before leaving her to her work. He really didn't expect her to answer in the affirmative.

"Yes." He stopped in his tracks and looked at her. "Possibly there's a little Reginald out there somewhere."

Russell stiffened. "What?"

The depth of Reginald's stupidity never ceased to amaze him. Or maybe it was just the prince's incredible ego that had allowed him to think that he could leave traces of his indiscretion right there, in his computer. This after he had gone through all the trouble, at Reginald's behest, of tracking the woman down to pay her off.

He did his best to appear surprised.

Strange how things turned out. Reginald's vanity could very well prove to be his saving grace. Reginald's unborn child was the natural heir to the throne. That could easily take him off the hook. With any luck, Weston could act as regent on behalf of the child until such time as the child was of an age to rule on his own. Anything was preferable to his having to be crowned, Russell thought.

And probably preferable to Reginald having taken the crown, he added as an afterthought. He had no doubts that, barring some miracle, Reginald would have made a terrible monarch.

Feigning surprise, he asked, "Who's the child's mother?"

"Strictly speaking, there is no child yet," Lucia informed him. "But the woman is pregnant. From all indications, by several months."

"And she claims that Reginald is the father." It wasn't exactly a question, but a statement that begged for a response.

"From what I saw in the e-mail, she's certain. Her name's Sydney Connor." She hit several keys on the laptop, then turned it around so that Russell could see the screen. "I was able to trace her e-mails to a computer back in Naessa."

"Naessa," he echoed.

Things were beginning to fall into place. Relations between the two countries were less than amicable. If he were to draw up a list of potential suspects who would have wanted to cause chaos within Silvershire by eliminating Reginald, the rival kingdom would be near the top. There were factions within Naessa, dangerous factions, that had aligned themselves with terrorist groups which had struck at Silvershire before and undoubtedly would again.

Was this woman working in conjunction with one of the terrorist groups? he wondered. "Do you know anything about this Sydney Connor?"

"Not yet," Lucia freely admitted. "But the day is still young. Give me a little time." She grinned. "A little bit of sugar wouldn't be out of line, either." Her grin broadened. "I run on sugar and coffee, in case you're interested."

"I'll have some coffee and pastries sent in immediately," he promised. "Would you prefer doughnuts, coffee cake or French pastries?"

"Yes," was her only response. Lucia turned her attention back to the laptop.

With a diet like that, he wondered how the woman managed to remain in the shape she was in. "I'll have them bring you a selection," he told her as he let himself out.

An heir. Reginald's "mistake" might now very well prove to be his own salvation. An heir meant that he wouldn't have to go through with the coronation.

He felt like a man who had just crawled out from beneath the crushing weight of a boulder. The relief was immeasurable.

Russell began to whistle while he walked.

Chapter 13

Russell stopped whistling.

He had realized, as he headed back to his quarters, that if there were an heir to the throne, if this woman, Sydney Connor, really was pregnant with Reginald's baby and if she could be found, then his coronation need not take place.

But, it suddenly occurred to him, if it didn't, what then would become of his union with Amelia? Would it be terminated, annulled, rescinded, as if it had never happened?

It was obvious that the only reason their wedding had gone off on the preset schedule, without missing so much as a beat, was because King Roman was anxious to have the treaty between their two countries go forward.

In that light, things had not changed all that much since ancient times. Countries still needed to forge alliances in order to survive. The strong protected the weak, not of out any sense of altruism, but because of the stakes involved. Two countries together were stronger than either country was on its own.

If an heir suddenly surfaced, and the line was restored to King Weston's house, then how would he, Russell, figure into all this? What would his role be? Would he even have a role, beyond that of political advisor? Since he would not be king, would Amelia's father call for an annulment and have her—what, pledged to a child? he wondered cynically.

Or would King Roman place pressure on his old friend and have Weston take Amelia as his wife? That was a possibility he hadn't even thought of until this moment. Weston had been without a queen these thirty years. The thought of having a beautiful young bride might be very appealing. It would go a long way to healing the wounds he now felt.

And where would Amelia weigh in on all this? Would she dutifully go along with whatever her father decided to do, for the "good of the kingdom?" Or would she ask her father to change his mind? To withdraw his negotiations? Would she demand not to be the pawn that she'd told him she felt herself to be in all of this?

He'd like to believe that she would, but he couldn't in all honesty be sure.

They had spent a wonderful night together that had seemed even better, if that were possible, than their first night had been. But that had to do with attraction, with chemistry, with emotions, none of which mattered when it came to the ultimate matters of state.

Russell shook his head. There were too many possibilities, too many uncertain elements. Too many "ifs" crowding his brain.

His good mood faded.

He held off saying anything to anyone about Lucia's findings for two days. And two nights. Two nights in which time and life were suspended as he found a perfect haven in the bed that had once been intended for Prince Reginald and his bride. The bed that was now his and Amelia's. He made love with her as if he was savoring a very precious, very fragile gift, never once telling Amelia that all this might be fleeting.

And then, on the morning of the third day, he couldn't put it off any longer. Slipping out of bed quietly in order not to wake Amelia, he quickly got dressed and left to see about business.

After first checking with Lucia to see if she had come up with anything further—she hadn't—he went to see the king. It was time Weston was apprised of the situation. Once Weston knew, the situation would be, more or less, taken out of Russell's hands.

His first loyalty had to be with the crown, Russell told himself, not with any feelings he might have. His was not to pick and choose, but to serve. If, after everything, it turned out that it was his destiny to be king, then so be it. But that eventuality might not ever take place.

And if that wound up costing him the woman that he had come to love with all his heart, that, too, was a matter of destiny.

Bracing himself for whatever the future had in store for him, Russell knocked on the door to the king's private quarters.

"They can't possibly think that we're actually responsible for this."

The protest, uttered in disgust, came from Nikolas Donovan. He was sitting on his small balcony that overlooked the sea, having breakfast alone. Only seagulls heard his words as he threw down the newspaper. A breeze ruffled the pages that came to rest on the round glass-top table. He hardly noticed.

The article that had stirred his ire dealt with the prince's resent death. It was the fifth in as many days. His death filled all the papers. Articles examining his life, his foibles and addictions, his lineage, abounded everywhere. Ad nauseum. Even if he'd liked the man, which he vehemently didn't, he would have been sick of him by now.

The article that had gotten to him dealt with speculation as to whether or not the cause of the prince's final curtain call from life was the result of an accident, or intentional. And if it was the latter, whose intention had been followed? The prince's or someone else's? Had the prince, the article demanded self-righteously, been the victim of some kind of plot?

If it was the latter, the article went on to say, then perhaps attention might be well drawn to the Union for Democracy.

Slate gray eyes had grown dangerously dark as Nikolas struggled with his temper. Rising, he shoved his hands into his pants and stared out at the sea.

Nikolas Donovan was the head of the Union for Democracy, an anti-monarchy organization that had been
in existence only a short amount of time, about five
years. But in that time, he was proud of the fact that no
one had resorted to any kind of actual violence.

Unlike the monarchy, he thought darkly.

It was because Silvershire was not a democratic state
that his own parents had been killed when he was a
baby. Killed by the man who now sat on the throne, he'd
been told by his uncle. Uncle Silas, his father's brother,
had raised him from the time he was a baby. It had been
Silas who had drummed into his head, for as long as he
could remember, that power belonged to the people,
not to one person solely because of the accident of birth.
Silas advocated a complete overthrow of the monarchy.

For his part, Nikolas was working to have a gradual
change come about. If nothing else, his group wanted
to get a stronger voice in the government. So that self-
absorbed narcissists like the late Prince Reginald did not
pose a threat to the common man.

His handsome features became almost dark as Nikolas's thoughts turned to the late prince. He'd known
Reginald personally. They were the same age and had,
Reginald by privilege and he by the sweat of his brow,
attended the same schools together. Their paths at Eton
and Oxford had crossed on occasion. But for the most
part, he was absorbed in his studies and Reginald had
been too busy bedding anything that moved.

Even back then, he had been a man with a mission.
That mission had been, and still was, to bring a better
form of government to his country.

However, that mission hadn't included killing the present-day crown prince, no matter how much he personally loathed and despised the man.

That the prince was dead evoked no sense of sorrow from him. Nikolas was certain that, had Reginald ascended to the throne, he would have abused his power, just as he had abused it as a young man at Oxford. There was no question in his mind that the country was definitely better off without him.

Russell, Duke of Carrington, the man who stood next in line, whose marriage to the Princess Amelia of Gastonia earlier this week had all but solidified the man's position in the scheme of things, was a better choice from what he knew of him, but still not the ideal one. The ideal choice would have been no king at all, because Silvershire deserved to be a democracy. A democracy where the people had a say in the government that ruled them.

He would go to his grave believing that.

In the last year, he had pulled out all the stops, urging anyone who would listen to join the movement, to make it bigger, stronger. A voice to be reckoned with. Presently, it was mostly comprised of people his own age and younger. The generation that had come before, ironically, his parents generation had they lived, believed in tradition, in maintaining the status quo. But they did not have as much at stake, as much to lose, as the younger generation did.

As he did, Nikolas thought. His generation was not complacent, would not go gentle into that good night like obedient sheep. Moreover, it was his dearest, heartfelt, fervent desire to avenge the death of his parents and make King Weston step down.

And have no man of royal blood step up to take his place.

He and his organization had stirred things up when they could, making people aware that they should demand a voice, a choice. The Union for Democracy had caused disruptions whenever they could to wake people up. But killing was another matter. He would have thought that had been made abundantly clear to anyone who knew of the group.

That the rumors even hinted that he and his followers were behind the prince's death was ridiculous. But he knew how these things spread. Knew, too, that it didn't take much to set people off against one another.

Though he didn't like the idea, he knew that he and his followers were going to have to be prepared for the worst.

Nikolas left the rest of his breakfast untouched as he went inside to see about getting together with his key people and making sure that the word went out that the Union for Democracy had nothing to do with the prince's death. Though he always advocated the mind over the sword, there was no place for martyrs in his plans. They had to be ready to fight if it came down to that.

In another town, the man whose neighbors knew him as Silas Donovan smiled to himself as he read the same article. It had begun. The unrest, the discord he'd hoped for, had plotted for and nurtured, was beginning.

He'd waited a very long time for this. Forever, it seemed. But revenge was finally taking form. Revenge against the man who had ruined his life. Who had taken his birthright. And the instrument he would use to bring it all about was a very personal one. When all was revealed, the significance would not be lost on Weston.

He could hardly wait.

Weston was grieving now. The so-called monarch would grieve even more very soon.

Silas Donovan began to laugh to himself. Anyone who would have heard him would have shivered from the malevolent sound.

King Weston looked at the young man before him for a long moment before finally responding. Grieving, still saying goodbye and unable to make himself give the order that would allow the autopsy to take place, the monarch was having trouble processing the information he had just been given.

It meant that he didn't have to say goodbye to his son. Not completely.

"A child, you say?"

Russell had begun to think that perhaps the monarch hadn't heard him. Since Reginald's death, Weston had withdrawn into himself to the point that there were times when he seemed to shut out the rest of the world entirely. He was a changed man, changed completely from the genial ruler he had been.

"Yes."

Weston took a breath, as if he'd been holding it, waiting for the right answer. "And it's Reginald's?"

Russell wanted to be completely honest with the king. That meant not giving the man any undue false hopes. "We're not sure of that yet. Ms. Cordez has managed to find only a handful of e-mails from the woman. It's going to take some time to put all the pieces of the puzzle together. And then, of course, there'll have to be DNA testing to substantiate her claim."

"Of course." Weston nodded. But the look in his eyes had become eager. It gave him a shred of hope, of something to hang on to. "Does anyone know who and where this woman is?"

"We know who, or at least the name she was using." The king looked at him, waiting. "Sydney Connor," he told the monarch. "But as to her whereabouts, again, we're not sure."

"Find her," Weston ordered.

The directive "immediately" was understood. Russell began to withdraw from the suite. "Yes, Your Majesty."

"Wait." Already at the door, Russell obediently turned around and waited for the king to speak. "You said something about 'the name she was using.'" The king furrowed his brow, concern marking his features. "Why wouldn't she be using her own name? Do you think this might be some kind of deception?"

The question struck Russell as odd. The king was usually sharper than this. "Your Majesty knows that royalty has always been the center of intrigue. Nothing is ever what it seems."

Eyes that were red-rimmed from tears met his. "You are."

Russell smiled. In all his years of service, and in the years that had come before that, when he had been Reginald's "chosen friend," he had not once ever lied, not once tried to present anything but the truth. "Thank you, Your Majesty, but I am the exception."

The king laughed at the simple remark. And then his features sobered until they bordered on grave. The monarch looked at him. "You realize that if there is a child and it is Reginald's and a male, then you won't be the next ruler of Silvershire."

Again, Russell inclined his head. The smile that was on his lips was not forced. It rose of its own volition. "Yes, I know."

A man completely devoid of ambition was rare. "And that would be all right with you?"

That would be perfect with him, Russell thought. Aloud, he said, "You might recall, Your Majesty, I never wanted to be king."

Weston was aware of that, but circumstances bring about changes, and desires flourish even in desert terrain.

"That is not what I am asking." The king paused. "Thirty years ago, I didn't want to be king, either. Not with as much resistance as I witnessed you originally display, but I had made peace with the fact that Vladimir would be king once King Dunford passed on the crown. Even though I didn't feel that Vladimir had the best interests of the people at heart, he would have had my allegiance.

"However, after my protests had been overridden and King Dunford gave the crown to me, I discovered that I liked being the king. Liked having the reins of the country in my hand. Liked the thought that perhaps I was helping the people I was serving. I knew in my heart that Vladimir would abuse his power, place himself first instead of in the service of his people, so initially I took it as my obligation."

For a moment, Weston allowed his thoughts drift to another time, a time when his hair was dark and his body firmer. When there had been a wife by his side and anything was possible.

"And eventually," he continued, looking at Russell, "I was glad I did. Eventually, I came to enjoy my lofty position. It is seductive in its own right, being king," he confided. "Now things are in place for your coronation and I want to know, if this child does exist and we do find it, how are you going to feel?" When Russell said nothing, Weston supplied a word for him. "Cheated?"

"Relieved," Russell finally countered after a moment had passed. "I have never in my life wanted to be the center of attention. I always did much better when I was allowed to work off to the side."

But the king heard only one thing. "There's hesitation in your voice, Carrington."

He couldn't dispute that. But he wasn't hesitating because he wanted the crown. Not for its own sake at any rate. "I was wondering…"

"Yes?"

There was no delicate way to broach this. Russell felt almost transparent as he asked, "If I am not to be king, will my union with the princess be annulled?"

The question caught Weston by surprise. "I hadn't thought of that. Under the circumstances, I don't believe so, but it would have to be discussed with King Roman." And then the thoughtful frown disappeared, to be replaced with a tickled laugh. "Forgive me, Carrington, but this is placing the horse before the cart. If there is a cart. If there is a horse," he added with a hopeful note.

To Russell's surprise, the king let out a long, soulful sigh. "I still cannot make myself believe that Reginald is actually gone. I miss him, Russell," he confided, his voice lowering to almost an intimate whisper. "Miss the thought of him, actually. Our paths did not really cross all that often these last few years." The king waved his hand vaguely about. "I was always involved in matters of state and he was always out, doing something," Weston's mouth twisted in an indulgent smile, "*unstatesmanlike* I suppose would be the best description of what he got himself into."

Russell felt for the man, but he knew that they had to move the investigation forward on all fronts. And the king had stymied one avenue. He began as gently as he could. "Your Majesty, about the autopsy—"

Momentarily lost in thought, in the possibility that Reginald had left behind a piece of himself, it took Weston a second to realize that Russell had allowed his voice to trail off. "Yes? What about it?"

Several people had put the question to him, asking him when the funeral was going to be held. The funeral couldn't be arranged until after the autopsy was performed. "I think we need to attend to that."

Weston looked away, gazed out the window, saw the years that had passed. "We will."

"Sooner rather than later, sire," Russell urged. "Arrangements need to be made for the funeral. I can handle that for you if you wish, but first—"

"I know, I know, the autopsy. Yes, you are correct, of

course. I'll give instructions about that presently, I give you my word." Turning from the window, he looked at Russell again. "A baby, you say?"

Russell smiled indulgently, knowing that he would not be leaving soon. "Yes, sire, a baby."

When Russell finally left the king's quarters some twenty minutes later, he was concerned about Weston's state of mind as well as the monarch's general health. The king, always so robust, so vibrant-looking, suddenly seemed to be wearing his years heavily. Russell knew it was the shock of the prince's death on top of his concerns about the state of unrest that was presently rocking Silvershire. The actions of the Union for Democracy had stepped up. Rumors of it coming to a head had been heard. He'd half expected something to take place during the wedding. The king had called in extra security around the palace just in case.

It seemed too much for one man to handle.

Reginald's autopsy was the immediate matter that really needed to be seen to, but there was no way to overrule the king. At first the delay had been because he had wanted his son's body to remain whole until after the wedding. Then the excuse was that he only wanted the royal medical examiner to perform the autopsy. Away on a short vacation, the doctor had turned around immediately and taken a flight back, only to be caught up in a temporary quarantine because two of the passengers on her return flight came down with a mysterious ailment. But she was here now, and still the autopsy was being delayed. He could only hope that the king's common sense would finally prevail.

Maybe news of the baby would finally get the king to move forward. Thank God Lazlo's operative was making some headway. The woman felt she was getting close to cracking the prince's code, which would open up the rest of the files to them and perhaps give them a better insight as to who might have wanted not merely to threaten the prince, but to actually carry out that threat.

And then there was the matter of the blackmail. Who and what was behind that?

He had a dozen questions and so far, no answers. He reminded himself that patience was a virtue, but he wasn't feeling very virtuous right now.

Amelia heard him before he even had a chance to enter the informal dining area within their quarters.

Her mouth curved. Strange how quickly she had gotten in tune with the sound of his steps. Her smile widened, its tributaries spreading out all through her.

Ironic, wasn't it? This was the first time that she was actually happy to be the princess of Gastonia. Not that she didn't love her country, but she could have loved it just as much if she'd been a commoner. But being the princess, with a princess's obligations, had, thanks to a twist of fate, allowed her to marry the man she had always secretly loved. Even despite all those strange little bugs that had come crawling out of her bed and the water balloons that had come flying almost out of nowhere during his visits.

She felt just a fleeting pinch of guilt at being happy

over Reginald's death, but then, she had to be realistic. The man would have made an awful ruler. His personality, that of a self-absorbed hedonist, was cast and set. There was absolutely no reason to believe that ascending the throne would have made Reginald behave in any other manner than he always had.

On the contrary, it might even have made him worse. No one in Silvershire would have been happy, least of all her.

Well, no one, she amended silently, but the women Reginald took to his bed and rewarded with trinkets for their favors.

"Good afternoon, my husband. It's about time you made a little time for me," she joked as she turned around.

The smile on her face froze when she saw the somber expression on Russell's face.

Chapter 14

"What's the matter?" The words slipped from her lips in slow motion as nerves began to knit themselves together and tighten.

Something was wrong, Amelia thought, looking at Russell. Something had changed since last night when, like all the other nights since the wedding, they had found a haven in each other's arms. Her mind stretched itself in several directions at the same time, searching for a reason for the somber expression on her husband's face.

Had he found out something more about Reginald's death? Had someone else been killed? Was there some kind of further trouble or intrigue brewing against the crown?

The burden of leadership weighed heavily on her shoulders. Concerns about subversive organizations and the havoc they could wreak were never all that far from her mind and especially now that she had become the wife of a man who was about to ascend the throne of Silvershire.

Heads of state were given to dark thoughts, even if they tried to maintain a light, gentle touch, she thought sadly, wishing it were otherwise. She had only to look to her father to know that.

Had her father's thoughts been lighter, more optimistic in nature, she knew that he would have not felt the need to forestall a possible and entirely theoretical attack from Naessa by marrying her off to the future king of a stronger, more powerful country. Within reason and adhering to the proper boundaries of the social world into which she had been born, Amelia felt that she might have been left to her own devices in choosing a mate. Possibly allowed to even follow her heart instead of an international game plan.

And she would have wound up exactly where she was, she thought, married to Russell, who was the man of her heart's choice.

Sometimes life arranged itself in mysterious ways, she mused.

Russell wasn't sure just how to say what he had to say. Never glib, he'd still been thought of as being diplomatic. It had always been his job to exercise damage control after Reginald had had one of his escapades. But when it came to matters that concerned him, his tongue felt as if it were bundled up in an overcoat that was two sizes too large.

So he picked his way slowly through what was suddenly a potential minefield to him. "Amelia, certain things have come to light."

She'd never seen him look like that before, as if *hope* were only a word to be found in a dictionary. Her heart felt like a solid lump of coal in her chest.

"Things?" she repeated, bracing herself for the worst. "What things? And why do you look as if you're about to tell me that my pardon has been revoked and that I am about to face a firing squad?"

He nearly smiled. Incredible how her exaggeration had almost hit the nail on the head. At least, as far as his own situation was concerned. She, of course, might have feelings of an entirely different nature if this baby did turn out to be Reginald's heir. If that caused their union to be rendered null and void, Amelia might not greet the news with a heavy heart. She might even, it occurred to him, be relieved.

He was quiet. More so than usual. This was a bad sign. Amelia tried not to let her imagination run away with her, but it wasn't easy. And there were no clues that she could discern in his eyes.

When she'd woken up this morning to find Russell gone, she'd just assumed that the new king-in-waiting was going about some sort of royal business. Taking the crown over from Weston required a great deal of transfer of information. And there was the coronation looming before them. The date had been changed, but still, it couldn't be in the too-distant future. There was a great deal that had to be attended to between then and now in order for Russell to become prepared for that auspicious occasion.

Unlike her, she thought ruefully. Her role in the upcoming coronation was merely decorative. Her only job was either to stand or to sit beside Russell and look proud, which she knew she could handle without being required to resort to any acting on her part, because she was proud, very proud. Proud of the man she had taken to her heart. Proud of the man that she knew he was. Russell was everything that Reginald had never been and, had he lived, she was fairly certain he would never have become. Honest, kind, loyal, Russell was the kind of man who was concerned about leaving the world a better place than when he had first entered it.

But the dark look on his face probably had nothing to do with the coronation.

Or did it? she suddenly wondered.

Talk to me, she all but screamed mentally. Out loud, she felt she had to prod him along. "Is this about Reginald?"

"In a way, yes." And then, in the light of the repercussions that would follow Reginald's thoughtless act, Russell amended his statement. "In a very large way, actually."

She didn't like the sound of that. Had she been alone, she might have sat down, braced herself before hearing more. But she had always prided herself on meeting adversity head-on, on "hanging tough" before a world that was quick to judge. And Russell, she reminded herself, had never seen her in action. She couldn't give in to weaker elements and show him that she was unnerved. He had to think of her as strong.

"Is he alive?" she finally asked in a hushed, disbelieving voice.

Had there been some mistake made earlier? Had the body that Russell found in Reginald's bed only resembled Reginald marginally? Was that what he was so obviously wrestling with telling her now?

Oh God, please don't let it be that. Don't let me have to marry Reginald, after all.

She'd hang tough, she promised herself. A marriage was a marriage and there was no way she was ever going to leave her marriage bed, no matter what Russell was about to tell her.

Stunned by the question, Russell looked at her incredulously. "You mean did he suddenly rise up from the dead? Reginald was many things in his lifetime, but a vampire was never one of them." Although, more than once, he'd heard the late prince referred to as a bloodsucking ghoul.

She cleared her throat, feeling a little foolish for being so skittish. "No, I just thought that maybe a mistake had been made in identifying the body."

"I was the one who found the body," he reminded her. "It was Reginald. No mistakes were made."

Outside, a cloud passed over the sun, suddenly making the room seem dark. She fervently hoped it wasn't an omen. Amelia drew her courage to her and demanded, "Then what is it that you're talking about? What has this to do with Reginald?"

He looked at her for a long moment, wondering what her reaction might be. Despite her words, did becoming a queen outweigh everything else for her? There was only one way to find out. "There might be an heir."

Confusion narrowed her eyes. "An heir?"

He felt a twinge of guilt for having kept this from her, but it hadn't been for long.

"The computer expert that was sent from the Lazlo Group discovered some personal correspondence on

Reginald's laptop from a woman claiming that she was pregnant with his baby." Russell couched his words carefully. "It could be a hoax—"

"Or, it could be true," Amelia countered pragmatically.

Very honestly, she was surprised that this was the first paternity claim to be made, and that there was only one. Reginald had gone around scattering his seed with abandon since he'd been in his teens. That this was the first so-called bastard that had surfaced was rather incredible.

Amelia paused for a moment, looking at Russell. He spoke to her as if she were his equal in this, instead of some hanger-on to be kept in the dark. She liked that.

She hadn't been wrong about him, she thought. Her heart had picked the right man to love.

"And if it is true," Russell continued, "if she does give birth and the child turns out to be a boy—" He paused, studying her face as he waited for the significance of what he was saying to set in.

It didn't take much to know where Russell was going with this, Amelia thought. "You're thinking he could be next in line, rather than you."

"Yes."

When she was a young girl, everything about her life seemed to be cast in stone. Things were fixed according to her father's word or to the traditions that seemed to rule so much of her life. Now, with this news, it felt as if everything was in flux and what she thought was stone was merely plaster of Paris, easily cracked. Easily shattered.

The crown was not yet on Russell's head and, if certain things came to pass, it might never be. She looked at Russell, trying to gauge what he was thinking. The man could play poker with the best of them, she decided. Had her kingdom's only income still been garnered from the casinos, he would have made a perfect symbol of the successful gambler.

"How does that make you feel?" she finally asked.

He answered her honestly. "Relieved—except…" Unable to finish, he looked at her.

"Except?" she prompted.

He was not one to wear his heart on his sleeve, but when it came to her, he found that he couldn't quite help himself. "Except for the fact that if this does come to light, your father might call for an annulment of our marriage."

"An annulment?" For the first time since Russell had entered the suite, she found herself laughing. Laughing so hard that her next few words were shaky as she uttered them. "Annulments are granted if the marriage isn't consummated. I think it's a little too late to call off the marriage using that as the excuse on record," she quipped. "We've 'consummated' this marriage a great many times as I recall." She put her hand on his shoulder to steady herself. "I'm afraid an annulment is out of the question, Russell."

He took her hand, about to brush it off. He found himself holding it instead. Wondering if he'd been a fool, thinking that he would be allowed to face eternity with her at his side.

"This isn't a laughing matter, Amelia. You know what I mean."

Amelia took a breath, doing her best to steady herself. But her cheeks refused to pull themselves into a serious expression no matter how much she told herself they should.

"Yes, I know what you mean and I beg to differ, Carrington. The day we cease to laugh is the day we begin to die. This most certainly is a laughing matter because, in case you hadn't noticed, I got the last laugh, so to speak." When he looked at her quizzically, she explained. "I didn't have to marry that horrible hedonist."

And then she stopped abruptly. Russell was looking at her as if he was trying to assess something. As if he was seeing her for the first time. Because she was so incredibly attuned to him, she suddenly realized what he had to be thinking. It hit her squarely in the pit of her stomach.

She might have been affronted, Amelia thought, if the thought wasn't so completely absurd, so foreign from anything she might have entertained.

Because she always tried to put the best possible face on everything, even an insult, she decided to take Russell's unwarranted suspicion, however fleeting, as a compliment to her ability to take care of herself.

"No, Russell, I didn't have Reginald killed, if that's what you're thinking. I would have had to take a number and I have never liked having to stand in line. My father once said that if I had to stand in line to get into heaven, I'd probably decide to go to hell instead." She cocked her head, studying his face. This wasn't all. "What else is bothering you?"

The thought that she might have had a hand in Reginald's demise had been a fleeting one at best. Though she didn't strike him as being a pushover, he knew she wasn't capable of coldly ordering someone's death.

He might as well get through all of it, he thought. "Our union only took place because your father believed I was the man Weston was selecting for the crown. If that crown goes to someone else, what then?"

She didn't see what the problem was, at least, not for them. Her father wouldn't be happy that the marriage did not back up their countries' alliance, but things did not always work themselves out perfectly no matter how much effort went into arrangements.

"Then you pledge your allegiance to the baby or whoever King Weston chooses and we return home to Gastonia to live happily ever after."

That didn't satisfy him. Hers was not the last word on the matter. "Won't your father want you to marry whoever is king here?"

Her laugh was soft, indulgent. She touched his face affectionately. "Not even my father would marry me to someone after I'd just been married before God and the good citizens of Silvershire, not to mention Madeline," she added with a broad smile. "That would be ludicrous."

"But the marriage was to reinforce the treaty," he insisted.

He was worried about that, she suddenly realized. Her heart grew warm. He was afraid she would have to walk out on him. As if that could ever be possible.

"My father's not that small a man," she assured him softly. "Having his daughter married to the Duke of Carrington, the king's right-hand political adviser, carries weight to it," she assured him, then added, "Especially when he sees how happy his daughter is—in direct contrast to how very unhappy he knew she would have been if Reginald had lived and he had become her husband."

A small wave of relief finally came. Russell allowed himself a small, affectionate smile. "You're referring to yourself in the third person."

Amelia pretended to toss her head. "All us royal types do that." And then she laughed and winked.

He put his hands on her waist, holding her for a moment, thinking how quickly he had gotten used to having her in his arms.

Again, his expression became somber as concern nibbled away at him. "But if it came to that, if your father decided that Gastonia's needs were immediate and urgent and since the heir to Silvershire's throne was an infant, perhaps a more suitable match for the matter of security could be made with the prince of another kingdom—" There were still a few kingdoms that could come into play when it came to making treaties, kingdoms that knew safety lay in alliances.

She didn't want to play this game. It was tiring and pointless. What he was suggesting wasn't going to happen. Amelia placed her finger to his lips, stilling them. "Don't borrow trouble, Your Highness. I'm your wife and I'm going to remain that way."

She'd called him "Your Highness," as if he were a prince. It was in jest, but he couldn't divorce himself from the thought that that was what she wanted from the man she was wed to. The promise of a crown.

His eyes searched her face as he asked, "Would it bother you if I wasn't king?"

"It wasn't your crown that drew me to you in the first

place," she reminded him, lacing her arms around his neck. She sighed as her body came in contact with his. "It won't be your crown that will make me want to remain."

"Oh?" The weightier matters of Reginald's death and the state of the country took a back seat to what was happening here, in this section of the palace. He felt his mouth curving into a smile, felt his body following suit. "And what will?"

Her arms still around his neck, Amelia pressed her body tightly up against his. Her eyes were dancing as she said, "Guess."

She could make him forget everything else in a heartbeat. He'd never met another woman like her and was grateful that somehow, fate had arranged for her to be his. "I had no idea that you were this lusty, Princess."

"Neither did I, Carrington," she teased, amusement highlighting her features. "See what you've done?"

"I?" he asked innocently.

"Yes, you." She raised herself up on her toes, bringing her mouth up close to his. "You've made a wanton woman out of me." She could feel love exuding from every pore of her body. It was incredible what a difference a few weeks made. Just a month ago, she'd seen her life—certainly her happiness—ending. And now, she could honestly say she had never been happier. All because she was married to Russell. "And then an honest one."

"I had nothing to do with that," he reminded her. "That was the king's choice. And, as for the first matter, as I remember the series of events, you were the one who chose me, not the other way around."

With a laugh filled with pleasure, she kissed him. She did it quickly, then did it again before drawing away, savoring the masculine taste of his lips. She could feel her blood singing.

"If they don't make you king, you could always become the royal lawyer," Amelia quipped. He reached for her, but she playfully took a step back, lacing her fingers through his hand. "Now, tell me everything. Just who is this woman who says she's having Reginald's baby? Do you know her? Do I?"

He drew her over to the sofa and sat down, pulling her onto his lap. She settled in, lacing her arms around his neck as she listened.

"No to both," he told her. "Unless it's an alias of some kind. According to what Lucia found out, the woman's name is Sydney Connor. The e-mail was tracked back to Naessa."

"Naessa," Amelia echoed incredulously. She banked down a shiver. There had been threats made against her father from several terrorist factions whose roots, it was discovered, ran deep in Naessa. "Nothing good ever comes from Naessa."

"Not so," he contradicted. When she looked at him quizzically, he said, "If this woman is on the level, then the future king of Silvershire might well be coming from there. If Sydney Connor is a native of Naessa, then Silvershire's new king would be half Naessian."

Amelia frowned as she turned the idea over in her head. There had been too much bad blood in the past between their two countries and Naessa.

"I don't think that's going to go over very well with

the people of Silvershire. Or with the people of Gastonia, for that matter," she added.

Russell nodded. She had a point, he supposed. For the sake of peace in the kingdom, Weston might not want to recognize a bastard's claim to the throne. It might set off too many diverse factions.

For the moment, his ascent to the throne seemed inevitable again.

"And it might just set off Nikolas Donovan and his little band of merrymakers," he commented dryly.

He could almost hear what the Union for Democracy would have to say about placing Reginald's illegitimate son on the throne. They could use the country's unrest to demand that the entire sum of governing power be turned over to the people.

Amelia put into words what he hadn't said. "And unless Reginald secretly married this woman, which I sincerely doubt, the fact that the baby is a bastard might make a great many people unwilling to accept that child as their king. For that matter, the king might chose not to recognize the baby, either," she added. "In any event, Weston still has the right to choose whomever he wants to be king since he no longer has a living son to take the crown."

Amelia smiled at him, her eyes encouraging. "I'm afraid that you are going to be king of Silvershire whether you like the idea or not, my sweet." She curled up in his lap. "Just think of me as your consolation prize."

"I think of you as the *only* prize," he answered just before he kissed her.

The kiss, meant to be fleeting as he stood up to take

his leave, took on a life of its own, growing and flowering until it threatened to overwhelm them both, blotting out the room, the palace and everything that was beyond the very small circle created by the two of them.

She heated his blood the way no other woman ever had before her. An eagerness went galloping through his veins, causing him mentally to discard the rest of the things he had intended on seeing to in the next few hours.

Nothing was nearly as important, nearly as pressing, as allowing himself to make love with this woman he had had the great fortune to have bestowed on him as his bride.

"Don't you have somewhere to be?" Amelia breathed against his mouth as he began to remove her clothing with the speed and dexterity of a finely skilled magician. Not to be outdone, she began separating him from his own garments almost as quickly as he was peeling her out of hers.

"Yes." His own breath was growing shorter and shorter just as his anticipation was steadily growing greater and greater. "I do. Right here," he told her. "Right now."

"Can't argue with that," she laughed softly.

And she didn't. Not for the next few hours.

Chapter 15

Russell turned his head toward the woman who somehow still managed to be a complete revelation to him. Amelia was in bed beside him. He had things he had to tend to. He knew they both did. But right now, nothing seemed to be as important to him as savoring this moment, lying here next to her.

"But you would be all right with that?" he asked, still wondering what he had ever done to deserve to be so lucky. "With the possibility of my not becoming the next King of Silvershire?"

Amelia turned so that her body was tucked against his. She smiled up into Russell's face, the warm glow of lovemaking still very tightly wrapped around her. They had already settled the matter, she thought. For all intents and purposes, it looked as if he were going to be the next king. But if he wasn't, she didn't care. Perhaps, she mused, she even liked it better that way. Because then they could go home.

"You're king of my heart, Russell, that's all that really matters to me." And then her smile faded just a little as a thought occurred to her.

Russell propped himself up on his elbow. He didn't like the way her brow furrowed. *Was* there an obstacle after all? "What?"

She picked her words carefully. The male ego, she knew, was a very fragile thing. Would his be bruised if the scenario he suggested really did play itself out? "If this does come about, if you're not crowned the King of Silvershire, would my being Queen of Gastonia some day bother you?"

Russell pressed his lips together, not to think, but to suppress the smile that rose to his lips. Titles had never mattered to him and he was comfortable enough in his own skin not to feel threatened by any she had. As long as she loved him. "You mean would it bother me to be a kept man?"

In her experience, men such as the ones he referred to idled away their time in vapid pursuits. That wasn't Russell.

"The only thing you would be 'kept' at is busy. Being the prince consort requires a great deal of work. You would be involved in guiding Gastonia, in keeping it safe. I don't intend to rule my country alone," she informed him. Amelia stroked his cheek lightly, feeling excitement taking hold again. "We are partners, you and I. Partners in everything that we do. Nothing would make my heart happier than returning to Gastonia. But I will not go without you," she added quietly. "And I will not remain there without you."

Russell turned his body until he was leaning over her again. He slipped his hand along her face, tracing its features slowly with his fingertips.

Amelia sighed just as her new husband brought his lips down to a breath away from hers. "I never believed in fairy tales," she told him. "Until now."

"Stick with me, Princess," he murmured. "The best is yet to be."

But the knock on the outer suite door, at first respectful, then louder, told them that whatever was to follow would have to wait. At least until they sent whoever was at the door away.

"Princess, are you in there?" There was no mistaking the urgency in Madeline's voice. It rang out, loud and clear. Her friend's tone gave no indication that she was about to go away.

Amelia exchanged glances with Russell. "Your lady-in-waiting apparently doesn't seem to want to live up to her title," he quipped.

Feeling protective of her friend, as well as somewhat frustrated, Amelia said, "Madeline has always had a mind of her own," just before she raised her voice so that Madeline could hear her through the door. "Yes, what is it, Madeline?" She glanced at Russell and smiled. He pressed a kiss to her throat, making her pulse jump. Oh, but she loved this man. "I'm…a little…busy…right now."

"Princess, the king is looking for your husband. I thought maybe he'd be in there with you." The smile that was in Madeline's voice said she knew exactly what was going on behind the closed doors. "King Weston requests that both of you meet with him at the royal clinic as soon as humanly possible."

At the mention of the clinic, Russell sat bolt upright, concerned. Thoughts of sharing another round of pleasure with Amelia were temporarily shelved. He reached for his clothing.

"Is the king ill?" he asked, raising his voice.

"I wouldn't know, Your Grace," Madeline answered. "He does not appear to be. But I'm just the messenger. One of several he requested look for you," she added.

Amelia scrambled out of bed. Russell paused a moment to let his eyes drift over her appreciatively. Rousing himself, he cleared his throat.

"Tell His Majesty that we'll be right there," he instructed. He allowed himself only a moment to fleetingly brush his lips over hers. "To be continued," he promised in a whisper.

"I will hold you to that," Amelia responded as she hurried into her clothes.

They lost no time in getting to the clinic. When they arrived, they found the king sitting in the corridor right before the entrance. The expression on his face was grave.

His complexion was far from viable, Russell noted. And the monarch's hands were clutching the chair's arms, his knuckles almost white from the effort.

"Is everything all right, Your Majesty?" Russell asked before Amelia had a chance to.

Apparently lost in thought, Weston raised his head

like one coming out of a deep trance. The monarch looked at him as if surprised to see that there was anyone else there. When he became aware of Amelia, he attempted a dignified smile to greet her.

"Hello, my dear." Weston shifted his eyes toward Russell. "And no, everything is not all right." A sigh escaped his lips. "My only son is being cut up." He struggled for strength to continue, to face the pain that seemed to be looming everywhere, waiting to ensnare him, to take him captive. "I've finally given permission for the autopsy to be done. You were right, of course," he told Russell without preamble. "We need to move forward, to get answers if we can. And to finally bury Prince Reginald the way he deserves to be buried."

Relief whispered through Russell. He was seriously beginning to worry about the king's mental state, afraid that the monarch was withdrawing more and more into himself. Since Reginald's death, he'd caught the king talking to himself on more than one occasion. In addition, he was concerned that the monarch might just decide to go ahead and hold the funeral, burying the prince without having the autopsy performed.

He knew that, from the king's standpoint, Reginald was dead and that discovering that his death had occurred naturally or at his own or another man's hand did not change the end result. Reginald was gone. He had feared that Weston would be overwhelmed with that glaring reality and that it would cause him to lose sight of the fact that they needed to know how.

"When did it begin? The autopsy," Amelia added gently, kneeling down beside the man who, even a few days earlier, had looked so dynamic, so bold, and who now seemed to be a shadow of his former self.

Grief had done that, she thought. Grief had hollowed him out until he appeared brittle and frail.

"Less than half an hour ago. I thought you should be here for the outcome," he murmured to Russell.

"We'll stay with you." Russell's eyes met Amelia's and she gave him a small, imperceptible nod in response. "Until it's over."

Gratitude came over the monarch's features. "I would be in debt to you for that," he told them, looking from one to the other. A little of his former self was restored, at least for the moment. "I know I should be strong enough to remain here, waiting to be told the results. But the image." His eyes looked haunted as he envisioned what was going on a few short feet from where he sat. "I can't get the image out of my head—" He swept his long fingers along his temples, as if trying to banish what he saw in his mind's eye, as if he felt an almost unbearable pounding. The king was suffering from headaches that were growing greater in number and more intense each time.

"We have nowhere else to be, Your Majesty," Amelia assured him gently. Smiling into his eyes, she laced her fingers through his. Weston looked at her as if seeing her for the first time. The gratitude in his eyes was all the thanks she needed.

The hands on the antique grandfather clock that stood a little way down the lavishly decorated corridor seemed to move at an inordinately slow pace. Russell wanted this to be over with, to have the autopsy completed and the king's son sewn back together again, to be a whole person again rather than the sum of parts that had been weighed, calibrated and measured.

Granted, he had been the one to lobby the king the hardest to have the autopsy performed, and they needed the answers that the autopsy would provide, but he had no idea he would be here, only a few feet away from the actual autopsy room, while the royal medical examiner performed her duties. Somehow, that seemed rather ghoulish to him.

A necessary evil, he told himself, glancing over toward the princess. He didn't have the right to complain, even silently. Just look at the hand that fate had dealt him.

Amelia had been carrying on a steady stream of conversation the entire time they'd been waiting, bless her, he thought. She seemed to know a little about everything. Right now, he and the king were being given a verbal tour of the factory where the Gaston, the car that had firmly placed Gastonia on the map as something other than just another collection of casinos, was manufactured. The king actually seemed mildly distracted, which he knew was Amelia's main, most likely only, goal.

And then, after what seemed like hours, the door opened and Dr. Abby Burnett came out. There was a grim expression on the physician's usually amiable, plain face.

Weston was on his feet immediately. The chair almost fell backwards from his momentum. "Well?" he asked eagerly. "Is the prince…?"

"Yes," Dr. Burnett told him. "I've just now finished stitching him back up." She pressed her lips together, obviously wrestling with something. She nodded at the chair behind him. "Your Majesty, perhaps you'd like to sit down."

Weston frowned, dismissing the suggestion. "I *have* been sitting down. Sitting down so long that I'm fairly certain I have permanently flattened your cushions." He drew his shoulders back, momentarily looking like the formidable ruler he had always been. "Now, out with it. What have you discovered?"

There was a wealth of information to dispense. The doctor picked her way through it carefully. "That your son did not die a natural death. That he didn't even die accidentally by his own hand."

"There was no drug overdose?" Weston made no effort to cover his eagerness for the confirmation. This, at least, would take his son out of the realm of being just another careless drug abuser. He didn't want that to be Reginald's legacy, that he'd died accidentally while seeking an artificial rush.

"Unless, of course," the medical examiner added dryly, "Prince Reginald intended to 'accidentally' poison himself."

"Poison?" Amelia echoed, trying to process the information.

She knew of the adult Reginald predominantly through what she had read in the newspapers and magazine. Even the most charitable, conservative accountings made the man out to be difficult to deal with. How many toes had Reginald stepped on, how many people had secretly plotted getting their revenge against him? It looked as if one of them had finally succeeded. But who?

Amelia glanced at her husband and wondered if they would ever get to the bottom of it or if this was destined to remain one of those unsolved mysteries that teased armchair detectives from time to time.

"Poison," the medical examiner repeated. Her tone left no room for argument.

"What kind of poison?" Russell wanted to know. If they knew what kind and its strength, maybe they could track down its purchase and with that, perhaps discover the name of the killer.

"Did he suffer?" Weston wanted to know before the medical examiner could answer Russell's question.

The look in the doctor's eyes told Russell that Dr. Burnett was torn. Torn between ethics and empathy. Between telling the king the truth and allowing the monarch to seek solace within a comforting lie.

But then the medical examiner raised her head as if she had made up her mind. Her expression told him that she was going with the truth. Lying, even for the best of reasons, would only undercut her ultimate value to the king. He had to be able to trust her. To know that he could believe what she told him.

The king was not a stupid man. Once the pain of hearing what she had to tell him had worked its way into the tapestry of his life, King Weston would realize that no one simply fell asleep after ingesting poison. That before death claimed the despairing soul seeking an end, there came the feeling of being strangled, of suddenly realizing that you were about to die and that there was nothing that could be done to avoid the inevitable.

Dr. Burnett placed a comforting hand on the monarch's shoulder. "Somewhat, I'm afraid."

Amelia slipped her hand into Weston's, pretending not to see the tears gathering in the man's eyes. "I'm so sorry, Your Majesty," she whispered.

"But there is something more."

Dr. Burnett's words sliced through the pain winding itself around his heart. Weston stared at her.

"More? The word no longer has any meaning to me, doctor. There is no 'more.' I've lost my son, my only son. For me, there is only less, not more."

"Well, Your Majesty," the medical examiner went on almost wearily, as if bracing herself for a very steep uphill climb, "that's just it."

"What's just it?" Russell asked, cutting in. He exchanged confused glances with Amelia, who shook her head, indicating that she had no more of a clue about what was going on than he did.

"It doesn't look as if you've really lost your only son," Dr. Burnett went on, only to have the king interrupt her again.

"What are you talking about?" Weston demanded. "You just dissected him in your clinic. You just came from there." He gestured toward the clinic's doors.

Dr. Burnett slipped her slender hands deep into the pockets of the lab coat she had thrown over her operating livery. "I dissected someone," she agreed, "but it wasn't your son."

Amelia was trying to make sense out of what was being told to them. "Someone switched the bodies?" she guessed incredulously.

Dr. Burnett's eyes shifted toward her. "Yes, but not right now."

"I don't understand," Russell interrupted. What she was suggesting wasn't possible. The clinic had been secured. The palace was always secured and never more so than now. No one short of a magician could have come in and switched the bodies before the autopsy. Besides, there was also the fact that Weston had just been with Reginald earlier today, paying his final respects. The doctor had to have made some mistake. "When could this so-called 'switch' have taken place?" he challenged.

Her answer floored them all. "My guess is thirty years ago. At the hospital right after the queen gave birth."

For the first time in days, color rose to the king's cheeks. "What are you talking about?" he demanded heatedly. "That isn't possible."

"I'm afraid that it is," Dr. Burnett said calmly. "That it has to be. There is no other explanation."

The calmer she sounded the more agitated Weston grew. "No other explanation for what?"

The medical examiner took a deep breath and began. "Your Majesty, as a matter of course, a blood panel and tox screen were performed on the sample of blood I took from the dead man."

"My son," Weston interjected sternly.

She nodded politely and went on. "For whatever reason, someone in the lab accidentally did blood typing, as well. The man on my autopsy table had type O negative blood. You and your late queen were both AB positive. There is no way that man in my clinic is a product of a union between you and the queen."

"Someone made a mistake," Weston insisted.

"No mistake, Your Majesty. I ran the second test myself." Dr. Burnett looked to Russell and Amelia for support before turning her attention back to the king. She remained unshakable in her conviction of the findings. "I have no idea why this was done or who was behind it, that's not my job. What I do know is that the man I performed an autopsy on wasn't your natural son and that if there was a switch—"

Russell cut in, as the full import of what the medical examiner was saying hit him, "Then the Prince of Silvershire is still out there somewhere."

"I have a son? Another son?" Weston looked like a man shell-shocked as the question dribbled from his lips in slow motion, just the same way his gaze drifted from the doctor to Russell. It was clear that he didn't know whether to be overjoyed or shattered by the news.

"No, not another son," the medical examiner corrected. "Your *only* son. I don't know who the man on my autopsy table actually is or was, but the fact remains that he couldn't have been your son."

"You're right," Amelia cut in, trying to come to grips with what the doctor had just told them. "If a switch was made, it had to have been done in the hospital. Most likely as soon as the newborn baby was taken from the queen to be cleaned up."

It all sounded so far-fetched, so unreal. "Why? Who?" Weston cried, stunned. He looked at Russell, wanting something logical to hold on to. Feeling like a man who had just been given hope and had his soul condemned at the same time, with the very same words.

The real prince was still alive. This meant that he couldn't take the crown, Russell realized. The thought brought with it a wave of energy that filled his heart. He didn't have to be king, didn't have to suffer through the kind of life that was examined and reexamined on a daily basis. The relief he felt was incredible.

"We don't know why or who yet," Russell told him, "but we *are* going to find out." He looked at the sovereign. "I promise you that, Your Majesty. We'll find out who he is and why he was taken. And why we haven't heard anything about it until now."

It would seem to him that if there was a royal abduction, whoever had done it would have tried to take advantage of the situation. Yet in thirty years, there hadn't been a single word about it. Not a demand for ransom or even a hint that it was done. Why?

He couldn't shake the feeling that something dire was about to happen.

Reginald's poisoning took on a different perspective. Perhaps it hadn't been done for some personal wrong. Perhaps poisoning the prince had been the first step in the present reign's undoing.

"Your Majesty?" Amelia prodded when the king made no reply. She slanted a glance toward Russell, concerned about the monarch's state of health. "Would you like to lie down?"

Very slowly, Weston turned his head toward her, as if unable to move his eyes independently. "I—I—"

He couldn't go on, couldn't force any more words from his lips. There was no air with which to move them. His heart was hammering too hard for him to catch his breath. What there was of it was quickly fading from him. And his head, his head was doing very strange things. Lights were winking in and out, blurring his vision, making him see things out of his past. Things that were not there.

A baby. His wife. Both appeared to him in flashes and then were gone. And all the while, there was this pounding in his brain. A pounding that grew ever louder.

Weston's knees gave way, failing him.

Like a crumpled doll, the king collapsed. He would have hit the floor had Russell's reflexes not been so keen. He grabbed the monarch just before the latter hit the floor.

Propping him up, Russell looked at the king. "Your Majesty, can you hear me?" Russell cried. Weston's eyes rolled back in his head.

Dr. Burnett was at his side immediately. "Bring him in here!" she ordered, leading the way into the clinic. Russell picked the unconscious man up in his arms and followed her. Amelia was right beside him.

An alarm was sounded. Instantly, there were technicians and equipment materializing from all over the fully stocked clinic. Russell placed the king down on the gurney that had been brought over, then stepped back. Amelia shadowed his movements, her eyes never leaving the king's crumpled body.

"Is he—?" She couldn't get herself to finish the question.

"He's still alive," Russell told her.

The staff did what they could. The defibrillator paddles were not necessary. The king's heart went on beating, but despite all their best efforts, the king remained unconscious.

Maybe it was better that way, Russell thought, watching as the king was taken to a private room. Everything that had happened in the last few minutes had been too much for the monarch to process. The man needed his rest. His body needed to fight its way back to health. To grow strong enough to handle the adverse situation it found itself in.

"Inform whoever needs to be told that the king is staying here tonight," Dr. Burnett told Russell.

"Do you think a hospital might be better for him?" Amelia suggested.

"The king has been fighting off the effects of the flu," the doctor told her. "We're running some tests, but perhaps all he needs is a little rest. We can tell more in the morning."

Russell nodded. In the meantime, he thought, he had answers to find and a potential king to track down.

"We're not going to Gastonia just yet," he told Amelia.

Gastonia's princess threaded her fingers through her husband's as the doctor drew a curtain around the king's bed. They would be going home soon enough, she promised herself. Right now, Russell needed to be here. Needed to stand by his king and help him. His sense of duty and responsibility were among the things she loved about him.

"I know," she murmured. Her tone told him he had her full support.

A man could not ask for more. Not even if he were a king.

* * * * *

Read on for a special sneak peek at
THE PRINCESS'S SECRET SCANDAL
by Karen Whiddon, the next exciting installment
in CAPTURING THE CROWN.
Available in May 2006.

Chapter 1

"Are you sure she's—?" Chase Savage broke off, stifling a curse.

A horn honked. Traffic inched slowly forward. He pressed the cell phone against his ear with one hand, keeping the other on the steering wheel while he negotiated the heavy downtown Silverton traffic.

"Yes, of course." His caller chuckled. "Isn't it obvious?"

Though he hated to point out the obvious, especially to his boss, as head of the Royal Publicity Department, Chase felt he must do so. "She's avoiding the reporters."

The all-important press. Couldn't live with them, couldn't live without them.

His Grace, Russell Southgate, III, Duke of Carrington and Chase's employer, made a rude sound. "For now. She's holding out. You know how the game is played. You've dealt with her kind before."

Chase sighed. At the ripe age of twenty-nine, he really *had* seen it all. There seemed to be an endless supply of royal groupies and hangers-on, all wanting something for nothing. Some craved sex, most sought money or a slight slice of fame. Royal fame. Which he knew could often be a royal pain in the ass.

"Are you certain Reginald didn't—"

"*His Highness* might be a prick, but he's still next in line for the throne. She's not just any groupie. Even if she is from the wrong side of the blanket, she's still daughter to Prince Kerwin of Naessa, you know that."

"She doesn't move in the usual circles. I've never met her."

"I know." Carrington sighed again. "Maybe that's what intrigued Reginald. Who knows? But this time, Reginald's mistake could have an enormous impact. Not just Silvershire is affected. The woman says she's pregnant, for God's sake. If this is not handled properly, the situation could become a political disaster." The duke muttered a particularly unroyal curse, making Chase grin. Unlike most of the royals he spent his time protecting, when Carrington let down his guard, he could be a regular guy. Almost.

"Get to her before she talks to the press. The damage she could do…" Chase could hear the other man shudder, even over the phone line.

"So you want me to 'handle' her?" As a huge blue SUV cut him off, Chase pressed on his horn. "How?"

"With style and class, as usual. Offer her money to

take her child and disappear. You can do it the way only you know how. I have confidence you'll do splendidly, as usual."

The rare compliment, coming from Carrington, told Chase more than anything how important this was. In the six years since Chase had moved up the ranks from royal bodyguard to publicist, Carrington had been a good employer and a fair boss. He'd been instrumental in Chase's career, taking an interest in the man and helping him navigate the sometimes intricate maze that comprised royal life.

Effortlessly and tirelessly making the royals look good had earned Chase a promotion to Head of Public Relations. The Wizard of PR, his staff called him. He sort of liked the name.

"I'm on my way to the Hotel Royale now." Chase consulted his watch, a Rolex which had been an expensive holiday gift Prince Reginald had given half the palace staff. "I should be there in, oh, thirty minutes or less."

"You'll handle this." It wasn't a question. Carrington rarely asked; he expected or demanded. And what he wanted, he got.

"Yes, I'll handle it. Never fear." Chase closed his cell phone and turned up the volume on the radio. He'd downloaded and burned a new CD of classic American rock last night. Aerosmith blasted over the speakers, making him grin. Stuck in traffic was as good a time as any to enjoy his favorite tunes.

He saw no need to plot a strategy—groupies were groupies. Once he started talking money to this woman, he anticipated a quick resolution.

Reaching the hotel, he eschewed the valet parking and drove into the parking garage himself. With the ever-vigilant press well aware of his every move, he didn't want to risk being seen.

The Hotel Royale had a back entrance, and he used it now. Carrington had given him the woman's room number, so he took the service elevator to the sixth floor. He encountered no one, not even hotel staff. Shifts were changing, and he anticipated another ten or fifteen minutes of privacy.

Moving silently on the plush carpeting, he found her room and shook his head. Her door was ajar, the deadbolt turned out to keep the heavy door from closing. Since maids often did this when cleaning the rooms, he wondered if he'd arrived too late.

Pulling the door open, he saw he had not. With her back to him, a slender woman with shoulder-length, cinnamon-colored hair was loading clothes into an open suitcase she'd placed on the bed.

"Not much of a princess," he drawled. "Where's your entourage? Sydney Conner, I presume?"

Her head snapped up. When she met his gaze, he felt an involuntary tightening low in his gut. Damn. She was heart-stoppingly gorgeous. He'd expected that. They all were.

But this woman was no flashy blonde, Prince Reginald's usual type. Her wealth of thick, silky hair framed a delicate, oval face. With her generous mouth, high cheekbones, and dark blue eyes, she had a serene, quiet sort of beauty, not at all what Chase would have expected from one of Prince Reginald's lovers.

Instant desire—fierce, intense, savage—made him draw a harsh, ragged breath.

Staring at him with wide eyes, she reached for the phone. Calling hotel security, no doubt.

"Wait." He held up his ID. "I'm with the palace."

Her full lips thinned. "Let me see."

He tossed it, surprised when she caught the laminated badge with one elegant, perfectly manicured hand. After she'd ascertained he really was whom he'd said he was, she replaced the phone in the cradle and narrowed her amazing eyes.

"I locked my door. How did you get in here?"

He gave her a slow smile, his PR smile. "Actually, your door was open. Rather careless, don't you think?"

That caught her off guard. Glancing at the door, she blinked, then frowned. "What can I do for you, Mr...." She studied the badge again, her lush lips curving in a rueful smile. "Savage? I'm on my way out, so this will have to be quick."

Again, when she looked at him, he felt that punch to the gut. This time, a flare of anger lanced through his lust.

She was good, he admitted grudgingly. Her every movement was elegant, sensual. Her appearance, from the cut of her expensive designer clothing to the pampered, creamy glow of her skin, spoke of wealth and breeding. Not your usual palace hanger-on at all.

But then, she *was* a princess.

"Where are you going?"

"That's none of your business," she told him, matching his cool tone. "Since I have little to do with the royal family of Silvershire these days, I don't understand why you're here. What do you want?"

He flashed her a hard look, belatedly remembering at the last moment to soften it with another smile. "As you saw from my ID, I'm with the royal publicity department. His Grace, the Duke of Carrington, sent me."

She stared, her emotions flashing across her mobile face. Hope, disbelief and a tentative joy chief among them. She read the badge one last time before handing it back to him.

"Reginald spoke to the duke?" she asked. "He told him about our baby?"

Hearing the raw emotion in her voice, Chase felt a flash of pity. The look she gave him told him she'd seen and hated both that and the fact she'd let her guard down enough to show her feelings to a total stranger.

Chase narrowed his eyes. "No, he didn't. However, Lord Carrington has learned of your claim."

"How? How'd he learn?"

He shrugged. "I wasn't informed."

"But Reginald—" She bit her lip.

"Reginald what?"

One hand instinctively went to her belly. *Protective.* He noted this and filed it away for future reference. "If Reginald didn't send you, what do you and/or Lord Carrington want with me?"

She was sleek and beautiful and sexy as hell. Chase could think of a thousand ways to answer that question, though he'd say none of them. He had a job to do.

He lifted his briefcase. "I've been authorized to offer you—"

The window exploded in a shower of glass.

"Get down!" He leapt at her.

Too stunned to react when he pushed her down, Sydney fell heavily, the man on top of her. Panicked, terrified the fall had hurt her unborn child, she fought to get up.

"Stay down," he snarled. "That was a gunshot."

"A gunshot? Why would someone shoot at me?"

When he looked at her, she saw a different man. Gone was the affable, smiling stranger. This man wore a grim face, a hard face, the kind of face she'd seen on her mother's bodyguards, hired mercenaries, for the most part. Dangerous men who played by their own set of rules.

"Who are you, really?" she whispered, still cradling her abdomen. "You might be in PR now, but I'm thinking you might have another job title, as well."

He looked away, climbing off her, still keeping low to the ground.

Another shot rang out, taking out what was left of the window.

He cursed. "That window—what's it face?"

Confused, she shook her head. "I'm not sure. I'm on the sixth floor. No view. All that's out there is the roof of one of the lower buildings." Then she realized what that meant. If she were to climb out her window, she'd be able to step without much discomfort onto the other roof.

The shooter was that close! She had to protect her baby.

"We've got to get out of here." He grabbed her hand, yanking her to her feet. "Stay low and follow me."

He started for the door.

She grabbed her purse. "I need my passport."

"Come on." Once they reached the hall, he turned left.

"The elevator's that way." She pointed right.

"We're taking the stairs. Hurry."

They hustled all the way down. Their footsteps clattered on the metal edges, echoing in the narrow stairway.

"Let's go. Through here." Tone low and urgent, he shepherded her out a door marked as an emergency exit, instantly setting off the hotel alarm. "Good, a distraction," he shouted over the clanging bell and whirring siren.

Outside, momentarily disoriented, Sydney stumbled, squinting into the bright sunlight. He gave her arm another tug, urging her on, past the line of parked cars on the curb.

"My cello." She suddenly remembered her beloved instrument. "I can't leave it. Go back and get it, please?"

"No. I'll buy you another."

"You don't understand. It's a Stradivarius, one of only sixty left in the world." She attempted in vain to pull herself free, knowing she personally couldn't go back after it. She had to protect her baby at all costs, even if that meant she lost Lady Swister, her cello. "Please," she repeated. "It will only take a moment."

Grim-faced, he stared, sending a chill of foreboding up her spine. "You want me to risk my life for an instrument?"

"A three-million-dollar instrument. Please." She gestured again. "We've obviously lost the shooter."

"For now." A muscle worked in his jaw. "How the hell did you get a three-million-dollar cello?"

"Reginald gave it to me. I—"

They both heard the sharp report of another shot. Seemingly at the same time, the side window of the car behind them shattered.

"Go. Now!" Not hesitating, he yanked her after him. They took off at a run, across the deserted street and into a narrow alley.

"But my cello…!"

"Forget the cello. This way."

"My rental car's closer." She pointed at the cute red Gaston Mini, parked near the corner. "Right there." Fishing the remote out of her purse, she punched the unlock button.

A second later, the car exploded.

The force of the blast knocked them both to the ground.

An instant, and then Chase yanked her to her feet. Dazed, she could only stare at the roaring inferno that, seconds before, had been her car.

"Are you all right?"

She blinked, looked down at her torn slacks and bloody knees. "I…I think so."

Sirens drowned out even the still-clanging hotel alarm. Any minute now, police, ambulance and fire trucks should careen around the corner.

"Good." He tugged at her arm. "Come on, then. Run!"

Another gunshot, uncomfortably close, took out another windshield.

"Come on."

They took off running. Several glances over her shoulder and she still couldn't see the gunman, or anyone in pursuit.

Still, she had to protect her baby.

"Don't look back. Just run!" He led her left, then right and left again, into a concrete parking garage. Their footsteps echoed as they ran toward a low-slung black Mercedes.

By the time he bundled her into the car, she was out of breath and panting. Another quick look assured her they hadn't been followed. "So far so good."

"They found your room and anticipated the door we'd exit," he muttered. "It's only a matter of time until they find us. We're not waiting around until they do."

Starting the engine without sparing her a second glance, he shoved into Reverse, backing so fast his tires squealed. Then he gunned the car forward. The powerful motor roared as they shot into the street. They careened around the corner, barreling toward the main thoroughfare.

Suddenly, she felt every cut, every bruise. Worse than that, her lower back hurt. Alarm flared through her. Had she injured her baby? Sydney cradled her abdomen, trying to regain her breath, her mind whirling.

"What?" Now he looked at her, his hazel eyes missing nothing. "Are you hurt?"

"No. Yes. I—I don't know." She bit her lip, both hands covering her still-flat abdomen. "I'm pregnant. I'm worried about my baby."

"You don't look pregnant." One hand on the steering wheel, he issued this observation in a bland, bored tone, as if he dealt every day with shootouts and chases. For all she knew, maybe he did.

"I'm barely eight weeks." Stiffening, she refused to

look at him again, glancing out the window as she finally took notice of her surroundings. They were heading away from downtown, toward the Silvershire International Airport. "Look, Mr. Savage…"

"Call me Chase."

She ignored him. "Mr. Savage. Where are we going?"

Instead of answering, he gave her another hard look. "Any idea who was shooting at you? And why?"

"No. I think it's more likely we got caught in the middle of someone else's troubles."

"Troubles?"

She waved her hand. "You know. Gang war or something. We were in the wrong place at the wrong time."

"Princess—"

"My name is Sydney."

"Sydney, then. They shot at you. No one else. You. Your car exploded. Or course this was aimed at you."

Lifting her chin, she considered his words. He was right. "Why? Why would anyone want to harm me?"

Keeping an eye on the rearview mirror, he took the exit that led to the airport. "You claim to be carrying the crown prince's child. You know there's a political firestorm going on now with those democracy advocates and all. That'd put you right in the middle of it."

"True. But Reginald and I aren't married. My baby is no threat to anyone."

"Yet," he said.

"Ever." Closing her mouth before she said too much more, Sydney caught sight of the Welcome to Silvershire International Airport sign. "Where are you taking me? Why the airport?"

For the first time since appearing in her doorway, he looked surprised. As though she should have known. "The royal jet is waiting."

"The royal jet?" A tentative spark of hope filled her. "Has he asked you to bring me to him?"

"Who?"

Impatient, she shifted in her seat. "Reginald, of course. My baby's father. Are you taking me to see him?"

There was no pity in the hard glance he shot her now.

"No," he said. Nothing more.

But then, what else could he say? Reginald had made it plain he didn't want her, or the unplanned baby she carried. She'd even learned he'd gotten engaged to a beautiful princess from Gastonia. He'd moved quickly, proving his words of love had been nothing but lies.

The knowledge shouldn't hurt so much, but it did. Mostly, she thought with a wry smile, because she'd unintentionally done the one thing she'd always sworn not to do. She'd inadvertently mimicked her mother's life.

When she looked up she realized Chase was watching her and most likely had misinterpreted her smile. No matter, she was going home to Naessa soon. Then, what he or anyone else in the country of Silvershire thought wouldn't matter a whit. Not at all.

She'd managed to do as her mother had done, but unlike her mother, she wouldn't ever call her baby a mistake. From now on, Sydney had a child to think of. From now on, her baby would always come first.

A quick glance at the handsome man beside her told her nothing. Chase Savage had protected her, but what were his real intentions?

They pulled up to an iron gate marked Private. Chase pushed a button on his console and the barricade swung open. Driving slowly through the rows of hangars, he punched in a number on his cell phone, a razor-thin model which looked like something out of a James Bond movie. He spoke a few terse words—not enough for her to glean the gist of the conversation—and snapped the metal phone closed.

"All settled," he said cheerfully. "I've gotten us emergency clearance." They turned right, into the airport's private section. Sydney had flown out of here before, as most of her friends' families were wealthy. Here, in various hangers, the rich kept their personal jets. No doubt the royal family had several.

"Emergency clearance for what?" she asked as they pulled up in front of a nondescript gray metal hangar. "If Reginald," she swallowed tightly as she spoke the name, "didn't send for me, then why'd you bring me here at all?"

He frowned. "I had to take you somewhere safe."

"Not really." Studying him, she wished she could read his closed expression. "I'm not your responsibility. As a matter of fact, why are you—head of Silvershire's Public Relations Department—here to begin with?"

For the first time since he'd appeared in her hotel room, cool, confident Chase Savage appeared at a loss for words.

She pressed her advantage. "You started to say something earlier, before the shooting started. You said you'd been authorized to do something. What was it?"

"Not now." He shook his head. "We'll discuss that later, once we're in the air."

"In the air to…?"

"I'm taking you home, to Naessa. You'll be safer there than here."

"Home?" Exactly where she wanted to go. Except… "I need my cello." The Strad could never be replaced.

"I'll send someone after your instrument," he promised. "The police should be there by now. They won't let anyone mess with it."

"I need to see a doctor and make sure everything is all right with the baby."

"You can do that once you get home. It's only a forty-five-minute flight to Naessa."

Something still bothered her, though she wasn't sure what. He'd addressed her every concern smoothly. Too smoothly. Maybe that was the problem.

She glanced around them. "This doesn't look like the royal hangar. Where's the Silvershire crest?"

Expression implacable, he shrugged. "The king won't allow that because of the danger from terrorists. The royal crest could act like a huge bull's-eye for undesirables."

He had a point, though she hated the word he'd used. *Undesirables.* In Naessa, as the king's unacknowledged daughter, she'd been called that and a lot worse. *Bastard* had been her mother's particular favorite. For a while, Francis had adopted it almost as a nickname, referring to Sydney as her bastard spawn, reminding her at an early age how she'd ruined her mother's life.

Sydney vowed that her child—son or daughter, whichever—would only enrich hers.

Chase got out of the car and crossed around the front to Sydney's side, opening her door and holding out his hand. She slipped her hand into his larger one, noting the calluses on his long, elegant fingers, and allowed him to help her from the low-slung car.

Staring up at his rugged face, Sydney wondered about his ancestry. Though he wore a well-cut, conservative suit, his shaggy hair and hawklike features made him appear dangerous. She wouldn't be surprised to learn he had a trace of pirate in him.

As if he'd read her thoughts, he smiled, stunning her. He really was, she noted abstractly, struggling to find her breath, quite beautiful. In a hard, rugged, utterly masculine way.

She reminded herself that beautiful men were bad news. Reginald had provided her with living proof of that.

Once he'd closed the door behind her with a quiet thunk, she had another round of misgivings and tugged her hand free. While a private jet was always more comfortable than commercial, she barely knew this man.

"We don't have time for this." He consulted his Rolex, shooting her a look of pure male exasperation.

The watch looked familiar. Ah, yes. Reginald had gifted some of his staff with similar watches for Christmas.

"Shall we go?"

Finally, she nodded.

Up the steps into the waiting jet they went. A short, blond man greeted them. Evidently, he was one of the pilots. He pulled the door closed before disappearing into the cockpit.

Sydney had time to note the jet's plush interior before one side of the hangar opened like a giant automatic garage door.

Chase barely glanced at her. "Buckle your seat belt."

His cell phone chirped. Immediately, he answered, turning away from her to try and conduct his business with a measure of privacy.

The plane began to taxi forward.

Chase closed his phone and then powered it off. When he looked at her, the dangerous mercenary had returned, full force.

"What is it?" she asked. Something, some wild suspicion, an absurdly ridiculous hope, made her ask, "Was that call from Reginald?"

His hazel gaze touched on her coolly. "Is that why you came to Silvershire? To see the prince?"

"Of course. I wanted him to look me in the face and tell me…"

"Tell you what?"

"Never mind." No way was she admitting to this man, this stranger, the depth of her shame. Reginald had pretended to love her. And now, when she carried his child, a baby they'd made together, he'd pretended he didn't know her. She sighed. "Forget I asked that. It was foolish of me."

Chase watched her a heartbeat longer, then he dipped his head, his hazel eyes shuttered.

Another thought occurred to her. "Is this plan to remove me from your country carried out at Reginald's direction?"

"No." He gave her a long, hard look. "This is entirely spur-of-the-moment. Not planned. After what happened back at the hotel, I had no choice. It's not safe for you in Silvershire. Especially now."

That caught her attention. "Especially now?"

"That phone call… Things have changed," Chase said softly, as though his words could hurt her.

"Why? What's happened?" She searched his hard, rugged face. "What are you not telling me?"

He took her hand and leaned forward, compassion turning his hazel eyes dark. "That phone call I just got? It was the Duke of Carrington, my boss. I'm sorry to have to tell you this, but Prince Reginald, the father of your unborn child, is dead."

ATHENA FORCE

CHOSEN FOR THEIR TALENTS.
TRAINED TO BE THE BEST.
EXPECTED TO CHANGE THE WORLD.

The women of Athena Academy are back.
Don't miss their compelling new adventures
as they reveal the truth about their founder's
unsolved murder—and provoke the wrath of a
cunning new enemy....

FLASHBACK
by Justine DAVIS
Available April 2006 at your favorite retail outlet.

MORE ATHENA ADVENTURES
COMING SOON:

Look-Alike by Meredith Fletcher, May 2006
Exclusive by Katherine Garbera, June 2006
Pawn by Carla Cassidy, July 2006
Comeback by Doranna Durgin, August 2006

If you enjoyed what you just read,
then we've got an offer you can't resist!

Take 2 bestselling love stories FREE!

Plus get a FREE surprise gift!